Sweep of Fury

Killer Jimmy Tucker wanted to die.

'Do it now, Gant,' he begged the stone-faced lawman. 'Don't let 'em swing me off their gallows. Just shoot me now!'

He was pleading with the wrong man. The Marshals' Manual was Gant's bible.

'The law says you're to hang, Tucker,' he pronounced, 'and I'll see you do it.'

'You ain't human, Gant!'

Gant nodded. Maybe Tucker was half-right but he'd still swing. The next badman to receive mercy from Marshal Gant would be the first.

Sweep of Fury

Dempsey Clay

A Black Horse Western

ROBERT HALE · LONDON

ISBN 978-0-7090-8799-1

Robert Hale Limited
Clerkenwell House
Clerkenwell Green
London EC1R 0HT

www.halebooks.com

Typeset by
Derek Doyle & Associates, Shaw Heath
Printed and bound in Great Britain by
CPI Antony Rowe, Chippenham and Eastbourne

ONE

THIS MAN
MUST HANG

Jimmy Tucker wanted to die.

The murder charge, the trial and the guilty verdict
followed by his wild flight and recapture, had turned
a twenty-year-old boy into an old man. And like most
old men he was now beyond caring, the only thing he
had left to hope for – a quick end.

'Do it now, Gant,' he begged. 'Don't haul me back
there to swing before the whole lousy town, man. Just
pull that trigger!'

He was pleading with the wrong man.

The Federal Marshals' Manual was Matt Gant's
bible. The lawman who'd run wild Jimmy down
couldn't even bend a rule, much less break one.
Gant's flinty face was as cold and changeless as the
Buntline Special in his hand as he replied.

'The law says you're to hang, Tucker, and hang you will. In Chisum.'

'Chisum? But they were all fixing to swing me in Sacramento City—' The fugitive's voice failed briefly. He cleared his throat and his voice came back, dry and bitter now. 'So . . . you'd go that far, Marshal!' he accused. 'You'd haul me all the way back home just to murder me in front of my friends . . . and Rebecca. Do you hate me that much?'

'I've got my reasons. Hate doesn't enter into it.'

'You're a liar! I can see the hate in your face right now.'

The boy's eyes blazed in the light of the single lamp which illuminated the old line-rider's shack where he'd been finally run to ground. His mouth twisted as though the words scalded his lips. 'Judas Priest man, how far can your lousy hate reach? It wasn't me who tried to cripple you!'

The lawman's face turned white. One step had him looming over the boy, six-gun upraised. But the blow never fell. His face still locked, Gant regained control by an act of will and was again master of himself when he inclined his head at the open doorway.

Shoulders sagging in submission, young Jimmy Tucker grabbed up his low-crowned gray hat and stepped out into the windy night.

The peace officer emerged behind him, the limp barely perceptible, as was generally the case. Folks back home had mostly forgotten by now that it had been Jimmy Tucker's old man, wild Shep, who'd drilled that bullet into the lawman's leg and almost put paid to his career.

Jimmy was convinced that it had not been his recent crime and escape that had set the iron marshal hunting him over so many gruelling weeks, but rather the legacy of hate for his old man and what he'd done to him in the past.

Bitterness etched the fugitive's face as the two mounted up then struck east across the lonesome Buckaroo Hills. Yet because he was still more a boy than a man, and on account boys can never surrender hope the way older men might, they'd not covered too many miles before the prisoner imagined he saw a faint glimmer of hope edging the dark clouds of his uncertain future.

He immediately began to grin, straightened in his saddle and looked back over his shoulder at his expressionless escort.

'You know, you ought to think some on this, Marshal. About hauling me back home to swing me, I mean. Hell, you should know better than anybody they simply ain't gonna let you swing me back there. That there town don't even believe in hanging.'

'That's just why I'm taking you there, killer. They're gonna learn to believe all over again in the law, justice and the rope for scum like you!'

Gant's voice carried such assurance that Jimmy Tucker's optimistic grin had vanished completely without trace as he turned to face the bleak miles ahead.

Senior Federal Marshal Bryce Shankland was standing framed in his office window in Sacramento City the next afternoon when orderly Pike James came into the room bearing a yellow telegraph slip. 'Wire for you from Marshal Gant, sir.'

Shankland turned quickly from the window which overlooked the depot's parade ground. A tall, lean man in his early fifties, the senior marshal had the quick step and briskly efficient manner of a much younger man. Without comment, he took the slip from the orderly and scanned it with sharp grey eyes. It read:

Fugitive Tucker in custody. Request permission to stage execution in Chisum as deterrent against further lawlessness in region. Wire reply care of Law Office, Chisum.

Gant

The marshal's eyes lifted slowly, then suddenly he smiled broadly.

'By glory – he did it!'

The orderly, a clear-eyed young Westerner with sandy hair and the beginnings of a feeble ginger mustache, smiled. 'You never had any real doubts that he would, did you, sir?'

Shankland smiled back. 'No, perhaps I didn't,

James. If Gant had failed to get his man, it would have been for the first time ever.'

'Second, sir.'

'What?'

'Jimmy Tucker's father, Marshal,' replied James, whose sharp brain contained a near-to-perfect reference file on all federal police officers operating out of Sacramento City. 'Gant ran Shep Tucker to ground in Chisum, but after he was shot it was Marshal Denner who finished the job.'

Shankland frowned. 'Don't you ever forget anything, James?'

The man they called Record Book shook his head soberly. 'Well, I try not to, sir.' Something in the younger man's tone caused Shankland to study him intently. Not only was James the senior marshal's orderly-cum-secretary, but he was regarded as one of the most astute and clever young men in the entire service. 'Are you trying to tell me something, mister? Seems your mention of Tucker's father sounded rather, well . . . pointed.'

'I merely felt the Shep Tucker incident should be kept in mind while you consider Gant's rather dangerous request, is all, sir.'

'Why?'

'It occurred to me that the marshal's stated reason for wanting to hang Jimmy Tucker in Chisum might not be his only one, Marshal. Chisum was the scene of Gant's one and only major failure, and I believe we both know that still rankles with him. Also, it's true that Chisum has long been a dark stain on the Territory's name and I don't doubt that, with his retirement imminent, Gant can see the wisdom in giving them all a lasting lesson in law and order. It could well be he sees this as an opportunity to erase what he considers that sole black mark on his personal record.'

The other was thoughtful for a moment before he replied.

'Even if Gant's motive is as you suggest, I think two other vital facts should also be considered.'

'Which are, Marshal?'

'First, this office and everyone connected with it owes debts to Gant we may never get to repay. The man has proven himself the finest officer ever to serve here. He is undeniably, for all his hard ways, an ornament to the service.'

'I don't think anybody would disagree with you on that, sir.'

'Well, that being so, I feel we're obliged to grant his wishes in this instance.'

'I suppose I must agree. But your second consideration, sir?'

The senior man strode to the larger colored map of Mescalero County occupying virtually all of the office's west wall. He jabbed at the area of the map that was bordered on the southern side by the spidery outline of the Funeral Mountains.

'Chisum, James,' he said harshly. 'The black mark on the Territory's reputation as you just reminded me. A haven for thieves and rustlers and all the human offal of that benighted county. Not only that, but it's also been a funeral ground for lawmen – a stench in the nostrils of decent men everywhere.'

Even conservative Pike James found himself unable to contest this description of Chisum. With its remoteness from Sacramento City and all major trails, the town was a lawless backwater which had long defied all attempts to bring it into line with other regions of Mescalero County. Any peace officer appointed to Chisum who survived one full month without getting shot at was automatically viewed as highly suspect by his commanding officer.

'Hang that killer right there in Chisum. . . ?' Shankland mused. He stood before his window in silence for a time, hands locked behind him, staring down into the parade ground and thinking hard. Finally he turned sharply, and said:

'You could very well be right, James. You mostly are, dammit. But, we must never lose sight of the fact that he's the finest officer we've ever had, and therefore we owe him a great deal.'

'I doubt anyone would disagree with that, sir.'

'Then we will repay him. Let him hang that damned young killer right there in Chisum and be done with it. There's never been a real outlaw hanged there, and perhaps that's what's wrong with the major black spot on our otherwise ever-improving reputation. There's nothing like the sight of some hardcase swinging in the breeze to put the

11

fear of God into the godless!'

'It could be a dangerous job, Marshal, even for Matt Gant.'

'Doubtless, doubtless. But do you know any man who might stand a better chance of success?'

'I don't know of any ten others, sir.'

'In that case . . . let the preparations be made. If Gant thinks he can succeed then that's good enough for me. Get a wire off to him immediately, James – and also alert that evil hangman. Er, where is Gotham right now anyway?'

'He's scheduled to swing Judah Henry in Dunstan the day after tomorrow, Marshal.'

'So . . . that would make it the best part of one week before he could reach Chisum. All right, get that message off and tell Marshal Cardinal to expect Gotham to leave Dunstan in time to do the rope job in Chisum.'

'Yes, sir,' James said briskly, and with a snappy salute, was gone.

Shankland returned to his huge map. He envisioned Chisum in his mind's eye – the weathered buildings, the gaunt, unpainted false-fronts and the vicious and embittered faces of its citizens. By contrast he pictured Matt Gant the peacemaker, straight of back and fearless of eye, meeting that rabble face-to-face and announcing he would hang young Jimmy Tucker right there in front of them all – and heaven help any man who tried to stop him!

The marshal truly believed Gant could do it –

maybe only Gant. Such was his confidence in his man. Yet as he stood lost in thought he found himself reflecting on James's theory on Gant, wondered if it was correct. Was it a desire for revenge against the lawbreakers who'd almost ended his career in its early days that motivated his top enforcer? Did his pride still suffer from what Shep Tucker had done to him there in Chisum five years ago in front of all those who hated and feared him?

Maybe so, the lawman conceded at length.

But his next thought was one he would never admit to anybody anyplace. He knew that, deep down, he wanted it to be revenge that had motivated his best man to hunt Tucker down relentlessly. If Gant was squaring accounts with the Tucker clan because one of them had almost cost him both career and life years ago, it would prove that the man some dubbed Stoneface Gant was human after all. This was something that even his admirer and defender Bryce Shankland sometimes seriously doubted.

TWO

A TOWN NAMED CHISUM

The hot day was dying in agony as the marshal and his prisoner caught their first glimpse of Chisum. A yellow sun still seared the towering ramparts of the Funeral Mountains, but it was gloomy on the shadowy plains where the river was a glowing snake of molten fire as it wound its eternal sluggish way through the mighty mountains.

It was over a year since the lawman had been to Chisum last, but his first distant glimpse of his destination told him it hadn't changed. Some places advanced, some just gasped and died, but there was a changeless quality about this ugly town crouched upon the banks of the River Taloga. An untidy sprawl of sun-bleached timbers, rusting roof iron, sprawled false-fronts and endless dust, Chisum had the look, smell and feel of a place slowly dying – or maybe simply just all out of luck.

The mare tossed her white-blazed head and picked up pace, sensing the end of the long trail. Gant patted the sweating neck then reached into the breast pocket of his dark coat searching for one of the crooked Mexican cigars he favoured.

He halted while he lighted the cheroot, turning his broad back against the hot evening wind to shield the tiny flame. The spurt of the match revealed intense blue eyes and the deep olive tan of his complexion, burned brown by too many border suns.

He regarded his prisoner with grudging interest. 'You surprise me, killer,' he grunted.

'Do tell.'

There had been little conversation during the heat-stricken journey to one of the ugliest corners of the county. The dedicated man of the law and the youthful outlaw shared few habits or interests.

'Uh-huh,' Gant said. 'All this way, and you didn't try and make one break.' His lips quirked. 'Maybe all those stories I heard about what a wild son-of-a-gun you are were just that. Stories.'

In the unevenly shadowed light the outlaw looked younger and more boyish even than his twenty years.

'If you want to believe that, go ahead, hotshot. Enjoy yourself. It could well be that enjoyment and good times for you might be pretty thin on the

15

ground . . . when we get there. . . .'

Gant just nodded. He already knew his prisoner was a tough one, far more so than appearances would indicate. He'd not given Tucker one whiff of hope throughout their gruelling journey to the scum capital of the southern provinces, and intended to maintain that strict control until his prisoner kicked his life away in the final embrace of Madam Hemp.

'Let's go,' he grunted, and the prisoner obediently heeled his mount into motion.

Tucker rode slumped forward, manacled hands resting on the pommel. He was of slender build with blond hair almost the same color as the lawman's. For a convicted killer and desperado, the clean-cut features were remarkably open, burned a deep brown by the southern sun.

Prior to being arrested, tried and found guilty of the murder of Hec Oliver, Tucker had operated a small cow-ranch at the base of the Funerals with his sister Rebecca. To the eyes of a stranger the man could scarcely have looked less like a killer. But not to Matt Gant. Once any man was found guilty by the law, the marshal from that moment on saw him as though branded with the mark of Cain.

Gant's alertness intensified as they crossed the rickety old bridge slung across the Taloga and now Chisum's crooked, wagon-rutted main stem stretched bleakly before them.

Bitter memories of this place stirred but nothing showed in his face, which could have been molded from iron. He saw Jimmy Tucker square his shoulders as towners emerged to stare. This killer had pride. He wouldn't give Chisum the satisfaction of seeing him led in like a whipped cur.

The plankwalks were growing crowded by the time the riders reached the shabby central square. The silent mob stood staring at the ramrod figure of the man with the brass badge pinned to his coat, then switched attention back to his prisoner. Hard faces, ugly faces, the faces of true mavericks and renegades. Here and there amongst the men he glimpsed the powdered and painted faces of hostile saloon girls, their gaudy hues lending flashes of color that contrasted vividly with the somber attire of the men.

Someone shouted an ugly word and somebody else sniggered. But it didn't catch on. This was local gun hero Jimmy Tucker returning home for his own execution – yet there wasn't a man, woman or hot-headed youth present who wasn't at least a little intimidated by the sight of the tall lawman. Some of them glimpsing Gant for the first time sensed instantly why he had been chosen for the task of escorting Jimmy home to keep a date with the hangman. Those who'd seen Gant before knew exactly what he was capable of. Almost to a man they stood in total silence, arms tightly folded, chewing on their hate but swallowing it instead of daring to spit it out. Or at least, not yet.

The riders were passing the blacksmith's where a muscular brute with hammer and tongs in hand stood glowering out from behind a crimson forge. New to the town, the smith growled at his striker, demanding to know who the star-packer was. When he had his answer the muscle man inflated his chest and was about to hurl an insult when Gant's stare fell directly upon him, causing him to begin to fidget, then sweat and at last to drop his gaze. A bystander sniggered, for the brawny blacksmith had acquired a reputation in just a few weeks in town, yet by the time the two riders had passed on by he'd been exposed as all mouth and nothing else, never to be taken seriously again.

But there were tougher men in this town, and a silent bunch comprising some six or seven of that breed began to drift towards the rickety jailhouse when Gant swung his horse's head in that direction.

The lawman's glance flicked over the group before settling upon the squat, sadly-neglected bulk of the jailhouse. He didn't turn his head as Jimmy Tucker spoke.

'You're a fool, Marshal, just like I said. These boys are pards of mine and they know I never killed Oliver. They hate lawdogs, and that goes double for the crooked kind, like you. I swear you'll be lucky if they let you even lock me up, let alone try to hang me.'

Without response Gant swung his horse into the jailhouse hitchrail and swung down almost smoothly. Almost. A few might have noticed the slight give in his right leg as he raised his boot to the bottom step of the jailhouse porch, where he turned to give the mob stare for stare.

'Marshal Gimp!'

For a moment, Gant went totally still. But no longer. Then he turned smoothly without any sign of a limp and reached up to help his prisoner down from his saddle. Stiff from the long miles, Tucker lurched a little before squaring his shoulders, then started up the steps with the lawman's iron hand on his elbow.

They halted on the top step. Several men now stood between them and the iron-barred door of the jailhouse.

'Move aside!'

Gant's voice carried authority yet not a towner moved.

'Are you loco bringin' Jimmy back here this way, Gant?' an angry voice yelled. 'You cravin' to die, you stiff-necked bastard?'

The lawman fixed his eye on the man who'd shouted. He was youthfully tall with a shock of thick ginger hair tumbling across a low brow. Vestry was a cowhand with a reputation as a drinker and brawler. He'd testified on Tucker's behalf during the murder trial up in Sacramento City where the prosecuting attorney had expertly exposed him as a phoney and a liar.

'Move, Vestry!' His voice was quiet, yet carried.

'Not until we know what you plan to do with our pard, lawdog!' a back-of-the-bunch redneck insisted.

Gant put a cold eye on the prisoner. 'You want your pards to end up inside with you – or worse? Tell them to back off.'

The prisoner faltered. He'd seen a lot of the badgeman recently – maybe too much. And yet he felt his courage stiffen as he ran his gaze over his pards – Rico, Jethro, Jacko and the others. Good men, and proven tough.

He squared his shoulders and lifted his jaw. 'Your problem not mine . . . big man!'

'Your call,' Gant murmured, then reached into the slash pocket of his vest and took out a key. Quickly he unlocked the chain holding the prisoner's cuffs, looped the chain around the hitchrail and locked it again. The key vanished back into his pocket and he nodded to the puzzled hardcases. 'Move or I'll move you.'

Response was immediate. Big Tom Jethro inflated his barrel chest, shot a 'watch this' glance at his companions then launched a headlong charge at the lawman, head down, fists windmilling.

Gant's right hand blurred and connected with a smack to drop the brawler in his tracks. Whether the kick in the slats he delivered was either spiteful or considered necessary to keep the man down, wasn't clear. But the moment Gant's boot made contact with Big Tom a howl went up from his henchmen and Vestry and Heath were lunging for the lawman even as Jethro fell.

Onlookers caught the glint of light on gun metal

and Vestry went reeling backwards with crimson spurting from a busted nose where the six-gun barrel made vicious contact. He was still falling when the sweeping six-gun collected Heath below the right ear and belted him clear off the porch, landing to smash through a hitchrail and cause a horse to jerk loose and bolt.

The entire incident lasted scant seconds yet the brawlers still on their feet were frozen in dumb shock as Gant advanced upon them and deliberately touched off a shot that drilled between Rico and Jacko, missing both by mere inches.

This was town-taming – Matt Gant style.

'Get the hell off this landing while you can still walk!'

The lawman sounded like he meant it, and moments later was alone on the decking with just his prisoner – a prisoner with no color in his face and looking more like the shaking shadow of a hardcase now.

Gant nodded then unlocked the prisoner's chain again and looped it over his left arm. He rapped on the scarred jailhouse door with the butt of his .45.

'Marshal Gant with prisoner! Open up!'

Silence. Gant struck the door again. 'Bragg! You in there? Open up.'

The outline of a pale, pop-eyed face showed in a window and moments later a bolt rasped, the door swung open and the town sheriff of Chisum stood there in his longjohns looking like some drunk who'd been roused from his sleep.

'M-Marshal Gant, sir,' he sputtered. He blinked owlishly. 'And . . . and Jimmy?'

Gant's nose crinkled as the combined stink of long-unwashed body and cheap whiskey hit. His gun muzzle jammed into a sagging gut, driving the sheriff back inside. Then Gant shoved his prisoner inside ahead of himself, followed him through and kicked the door shut behind him.

The ten minutes that followed were rough on Sheriff Mel Bragg. First he was ordered to wash and dress, then was made to sweep out the office, starting with the cell that was to hold the marshal's prisoner.

Later, when the prisoner was securely locked in the cell that would be his last dwelling place before they dragged him out and hanged him, Bragg was set busy emptying his stash of three bottles of rye whiskey into the yard in back, after which he broke out the dusty jailhouse ledger in which the marshal made out an official entry pertaining to the arrival here – on this day's date – of one Jimmy Tucker, convicted killer.

Later as Gant sat at the desk writing with a firm, strong hand, Bragg was occupied scrubbing filthy window panes down with swabs of cotton waste. The sheriff was breathing hard. He'd not expended so much energy since Tom Bible's gang had last come to town and chased him up and down Trail Street seeing who could put a .45 bullet closest to his desperately flying feet.

Bragg had been scared that memorable night but was even more so now.

He was terrified to think how the town might react once the news of Jimmy Tucker's return and pending execution fully sank in.

He was unsure how the prisoner's many friends might react, and actually trembled whenever he tried to picture Tom Bible's response when he learned what was taking place.

These were scary considerations yet still less unsettling than the formidable man now seated opposite in his battered horsehide chair. He was one relieved turnkey when, after a time, Gant glanced up from his writing and ordered him down to the telegraph office to enquire if there was a wire for him there.

It was twenty minutes and two double ryes later when the sheriff returned to the office. Gant had lit the office lamp as well as the corridor lanterns which illuminated the two cells. The marshal stood with his back against the empty rifle rack, smoking one of his powerful black cheroots.

Bragg's hand shook noticeably as he proffered the brown envelope. 'Lester told me this come in about an hour back, Marshal. Seems to think it could be important.'

'We'll see.'

Cigar between his teeth the marshal tore the envelope and scanned the enclosed telegraph slip.

23

The ghost of a smile touched his lips.

'Good news, Marshal?'

'I believe so, Sheriff. But for you and your town – perhaps not so good.'

He slipped the envelope into his breast pocket and took the stogie from between his teeth.

'I intend to deliver a public statement, Sheriff Bragg. Have the citizens assemble out front in ten minutes. You can warn them that anyone who doesn't turn up may draw a night in my cells. Oh, yes, and emphasize that what they will hear will be of great importance.'

Bragg left, full of curiosity and scratching his ribs. With only the hint of a limp, Gant made his way along the cell corridor a short time later. Jimmy Tucker lay on his back on a narrow bunk smoking a cigarette and studying the tips of his boots. Gant stared at him through the bars and the prisoner met his look calmly.

'Somethin' on your mind, Marshal?'

'News, Tucker, news. I reckoned you should be first here to know that I've received official permission to stage your execution right here in Chisum. Milton Gotham, the Territorial hangman, is due to arrive within a matter of days.'

Tucker swung booted feet to the floor. If the marshal's announcement had shaken him at all he gave no sign. He rose and crossed to the barred door, leant lightly against it.

'You really figure it will work, Marshal?'

24

'Will what work?'

'Hell, this caper of tryin' to hang me down here, of course. You don't really believe you swingin' me out back is goin' to make folks forget that my old man gunfought you fair and square down here five years back and gave you that gimp leg, do you? And, let's be honest. That's why you've gone to all this trouble, ain't it, Marshal? To wipe that slate clean – at last!'

The lawman's jaw lifted.

'None of this has anything to do with your old man, mister. Shep Tucker was a back-shooter, a thief and a jailbird, and he paid the full penalty for his crimes. If he's to be remembered at all for anything it should be for the fact that he passed his bad blood on to you.'

Tucker nodded gravely. 'You really believe that crap, don't you, Gant? My old man was no good, so that makes me no good too.'

'The record speaks for itself. Shep Tucker convicted murderer, 1878; his son convicted for murder, 1883. Don't blame me . . . try blaming the evidence in black and white for the whole goddamn world to see.'

The prisoner rose and began pacing his cell. Tucker moved like a big cat. He was one of the quickest men the lawman had ever seen.

'It must be great to have everythin' so cut and dried in your head the way you have, Gant. You never doubt you could be wrong about anythin', do you?

You wouldn't even believe I was innocent of this crummy charge even if I proved it to you.'

'I deal with the law, Tucker, that thing that's bigger and stronger than all of us,' Gant retorted forcefully. 'The law found you guilty and it was my job to bring you in when you escaped custody, and now it's also my job to hang you. Where's the room for doubt there?'

'Nowhere . . . standin' in your boots, maybe. But you are still fixin' to hang an innocent man.'

Gant hooked his thumbs in his vest pockets and squared big shoulders.

'You are singing a different tune now, mister. Before this, you bragged I'd never catch you. When I did, you start claiming you're innocent. Why the change? Grabbing at straws and getting desperate and scared, maybe? Could it be that what happened out on the porch maybe put the notion in your head that your back-shooting pals won't be able to help you this time around?'

'That? Hell, you've just won a poker hand out there, Marshal. The high-stake big game ain't even half-started yet. You got one hell of a lot more to fret about than them fellers you call my pards.'

'Are you saying they're not?'

'They're just fellas I drank with and used to horse around with some when I came to town. But that was only once every few months or so. I'm a country boy, Marshal. Towns make me uncomfortable, and this town more than any other, I reckon. I never did like

Chisum, and I reckon if it comes right down to cases, I never much liked anyone who came from here neither.'

'Then why did those men try to stop me from bringing you in?'

The young man laughed. 'Lawman, they'd do that much for anybody. It ain't because they like me, lawman . . . they just naturally hate you and your kind.'

Gant nodded after a thoughtful moment. 'Well, maybe you're right. But I can say that kind of hate doesn't trouble me any. In truth, when it comes to scum like that, I relish it. For while they're busy hating your guts, they learn respect, Tucker. Respect for the badge and the power behind it.'

The boy's eyes tightened.

'Well, mebbe you'll get the respect you crave from the town, lawman, but not from me. And don't think death will change anything. If you do get to stand me on a gallows, before Gotham hauls that hood over my head, remember this. It won't be you standing there lookin' at a killer, but the other way round, on account that's all you ever were or will be, like everybody knows!'

There was passionate conviction in Tucker's words, yet they left the lawman unmoved. 'Your old man went to the gallows declaring his innocence,' he said coldly. 'Like father, like son!'

Tucker made to respond then broke off, cocking his head to the sudden sound of voices from the street. 'What's that. . . ?' he muttered. Then, 'Hey . . . sounds like a mob!'

'Just your friends, Tucker, just your friends. They've gathered to hear the news on you personal.'

The prisoner's eyes widened. 'You're sayin' you called them together to let them hear what you've got in mind? You must be loco. They'll eat you alive!'

'They'll find the chewing mighty tough, gunboy,' Gant stated coldly and, turning, walked back to the law office.

They were ranged up before the jailhouse in a wide semi-circle, some thirty-odd grim-faced men, with a sprinkling of painted doxies from the Lady Jane and the Last Hope adding a little color. The hot night wind swirled dust through the mob and the early moon, peering over the false-front of Parnell's Mercantile, winked softly from gunbelts, watch chains and cartridge rims.

A hush descended as the square-shouldered figure appeared in the rectangle of the jailhouse doorway, the angry buzz breaking out only when Gant moved out to stand alone on the top step.

Bragg came shuffling forward, breathing noisily through his mouth, brute face glistening with sweat. The man glanced back over his shoulder as he climbed the steps, then tripped and almost bumped into the marshal.

'This is plum loco, Marshal,' the sheriff panted. 'They've been knockin' the hard stuff back by the gallon and talkin' up a storm. They—'

'Thank you, Sheriff Bragg. Now get inside.'

Bragg made to protest. But then he paused to glance around, realized just how sizable the mob really was and suffered a sudden change of mind. He scurried inside with such awkward haste that somebody laughed loudly, a harsh, brutal sound.

Then somebody yelled, 'Well, say your stinkin' piece, Gant! We ain't got all damned night!'

Supporting voices rose on all sides, but Gant stood in silence, thumbs hooked in vest pockets, the breeze toying with his thick fair hair. There were angry shouts and one booming back-of-the-mob yell: 'Shake it up, Marshal Gimp, why don't you?'

They expected a reaction. When they didn't get one some of the heat seemed to go out of them. Gant remained staring down at them flatly, silent and unmoving as the voices faded off to a mere murmur until eventually it was all quiet on Trail Street but for the tinkling of the piano from the Last Hope Saloon.

Deliberately slow, Gant drew a cheroot from his breast pocket and set it between his teeth. He produced vestas, struck a light and set it to the weed. He flicked the dead match away, every movement slow and deliberate. This was a familiar role for the town-tamer and he played it well. Finally he spoke:

'Listen! One month ago, Jimmy Tucker shot and killed Hec Oliver of the Cross Bar Ranch. He was arrested by a federal marshal, tried by a jury of his peers in Sacramento City, and found guilty. The night before he was due to be executed, he escaped custody. I was sent after him, and I found him and arrested him. Naturally the sentence of death still stands. This man is to be hanged, gentlemen, as judge and jurymen decreed.' He paused, then added deliberately, 'He will hang here!'

Half a hundred faces stared back at him. At the bars and on street corners over the past half-hour, they'd proclaimed Marshal Gant must be tired of living to bring Jimmy Tucker back to his home town at a time like this. There had been any amount of wild and violent talk about marching on the jailhouse *en masse*, grinding the town lawman underfoot and setting handsome young Jimmy free. At that point nobody had dreamed the lawman might attempt to swing Tucker here in Chisum; many still found it hard to believe they were hearing right.

Suddenly the men in the forefront of the surging mob propped sharply. The marshal had dropped his hand to the handle of the Buntline Special. But pressure from behind forced them on. They leaned back in alarm, boot-heels ploughing the deep dust. They were within mere feet of the jailhouse steps when Gant triggered a single shot into the air, bringing them to a lurching halt.

Moments of uncertainty followed before something flashed through the air and a large stone thudded onto the porch boards.

Again Gant's shooter roared and an ugly man towards the back of the mob screamed, staggered and clutched a bloodied shoulder.

'Back up!'

Gant's powerful voice rose above the rever-berating echoes of the gunshot, beating against the false-fronts. 'If I have to shoot again someone will surely die!'

He meant it. They could tell. And in that moment the growling beast that was the mob was transformed back into merely a bunch of cowhands, day laborers, barroom sweepings and losers suddenly trying to make themselves invisible.

They moved back slowly and awkwardly as Gant rammed his gun back into leather. Then, to their astonishment, he started down the steps until he stood amongst them in the street so close they could reach out and touch him if they dared.

None did so. In that moment Marshal Matt Gant looked as big a man as they had ever seen as he stared coldly from face to face.

'Vermin!'

His voice rang gunshot-loud and for the moment he held them silent and fearful both by his contempt and his courage. But it would only be for the moment, and nobody understood that better than Matt Gant as he leapt atop a packing crate to carry the fight to the enemy.

THREE

THE VIOLENT MEN

'You're not denying what I say because you know it's true!' Gant accused. 'Just as I know that I am the law. I know it and you had better understand it. The law has come to Chisum! I can see some of you swallowing the notion already, and the rest of you will do the same after you see Tucker hang.'

'Never!' a whiskey-laced voice roared from the rear of the threatening mob. But the cry wasn't taken up. Too many citizens were standing too close to Matt Gant, and there was something about him that threw a scare into a man.

'Hang he surely will,' he reiterated. 'But a word of warning to any man who might think of coming against me. Just remember that in doing so you would be coming against the law. And the law I represent can be as merciless as it is just. If any man

32

challenges me, I will either arrest him or shoot him. No other options. Is that clear?'

'Oh – we all know you are some hotshot killer, Gant!' a muffled voice said from the outer edge of the mob.

A cold smile twisted the lawman's lips.

'Ah . . . the voice from back . . . always from the back.' He sobered. 'Well, if any man has the guts to make a point openly, I give my word I'll give him a fair hearing and not hold it against him. Now, that is – not later. Well?'

No man spoke.

Gant's eye singled out a husky individual in a faded pink shirt, arms like a buck navvy. 'You?'

The big head shook. 'Not me.'

Gant moved forward and the mob split before him. He halted before a short man with a black beard and the mean, close-set eyes of a ferret.

'You?'

The man compressed his lips but didn't reply.

'I asked you a question, runt. Don't you have anything to say?'

'No.' The voice was barely audible, yet had been bellowing mere moments before. 'N-not me, Marshal.'

Gant gave a contemptuous grunt and shouldered his way deeper into the mob. It was over twenty strong. He was taking a risk and knew it. But he kept moving in, staring this man closely in the face, then the next one when the first failed to react.

He propped at a movement in back of him and whirled to see the little man approaching, propping along on a crutch he had carried since a ball had taken away his leg at the Battle of Shiloh. He was leathered and wrinkled, with long grey hair that flowed over the shoulders of his tightly buttoned black coat. He halted and appeared anything but afraid.

'I have something to say, Marshal Gant.'

Lines of contempt scored the lawman's flat cheeks.

'Ahh, Judge Nimrod, doyen of the bench, counsel of the working class – advocate of thieves! It's been a time, Judge!'

The intelligent, gray face darkened. 'I see you are still as iron-mouthed as ever, Marshal Gant. And vain, I note. Yes, I suspect your arrogance may well have expanded since we last met, rather than diminished as it may well have done in a better man. Still wrongly attempting to walk taller than any man has the right, I see.'

'I do what I do in the name of the law – and my jurisdiction is in writing, should anyone query it.'

The man sneered.

'You . . . with that gun of yours, pitted against everyday working men who wouldn't stand a fair chance against you in combat even if they were put behind a loaded machine gun! Is this town to be Dalton all over again?'

Matt Gant sucked in a deep breath. He'd tamed

the wild herd-drivers in Dalton with his authority, with his understanding of the law . . . and with a Colt .45. Judge Nimrod had presided over the bench during that bloody period in rip-roaring Dalton, and they were bitter enemies from the first day to the last.

Whiskey and rum had come close to forcing the judge from the bench several times in Dalton, yet somehow he'd survived and now hung his shingle in Chisum.

'Dalton has been a peaceful town ever since I quit there, old man.' Gant's jaws were hard. 'As this town will be when I go. And if you begin meddling and—'

'Threats already, Marshal?' the judge cut in. 'You should remember they never intimidated me before.'

'Then does that mean you'll be opposed to law and order?'

'If you are law and order, sir' – the judge overode him – 'then heaven help us all. For the ways of achieving that admirable outcome have never been yours. Instead of seeking the peaceful gradual way to that goal, you employ force, arrogance and the gun . . . oh, yes, let us never forget that the Gant route to peace and harmony can easily be mistaken for a declaration of war. Your very manner, sir, is a goad to a proud man, and when that man reacts by coming against you, your response? Shoot them down. That is not law, and never shall be. What it leads to, is anarchy.'

'Finished?'

The old man licked dry lips. 'For the moment, yes.'

'Well, thank you, Judge Nimrod. And the very next time I feel the need of expert advice in how one man should handle five hundred brawling, lawless drunks some Saturday night – as I might easily find myself doing here – be sure I'll see your counsel.'

Gant swung his back upon the man. 'All right, I've had my say for now. Clear this street!'

They began moving away slowly and reluctantly, washing away across Trail Street to be swallowed eventually by the welcoming batwings of the Lady Jane and the Last Hope. Until, in the end, there were but two men left: Matt Gant, staring bleakly across at the stone horse trough where Shep Tucker's bullet had felled him five years earlier . . . and Judge Nimrod frowning pensively at his broad back.

Then, following Gant's line of sight, the older man said quietly, 'You've never forgiven him for what he did to you, have you, Marshal? Nor any of us?'

Matt Gant turned slowly, muscles working his lean jawline. 'I said I'd come to you if I needed the benefit of your whiskey-addled tongue, Judge, not before!'

'Pride, Marshal, pride. Pride one day must oversee its own fall.'

'I only hope I never fall as far as you have already.'

Stung, the judge retorted, 'Damn it but you still hold yourself higher than any man has the right, Marshal.' He leaned forward on his crutch, eyes blazing. 'What is it like, Marshal? Tell me what it is like to be man and god all at once?'

The marshal's face was cold as he replied. 'I wouldn't know, Judge. What's it like to be neither?'

Gant stood on the shadowed porch of the hardware store looking over Trail Street. His long night at the jailhouse had passed without incident. His eyes felt gritty from lack of sleep but the meal he'd had Bragg fetch him in from the Diamond Spot Café an hour back had counteracted the weariness. He was clean-shaven. His dark suit was freshly brushed and his flat-brimmed hat was slanted at exactly the right angle upon his large head.

It was around ten and Chisum was going about its normal activities. Women browsed at store windows. A loaded buckboard rolled noisily down the main stem. Directly across from him, a short, fat man wearing bright red sleeve guards was washing down the windows of the pastry shop. Few porch loafers were abroad as yet. The lights of the Lady Jane and the Last Hope had burned late into the night while men swigged whiskey and talked about the biggest thing that had happened in Chisum in years – the town-tamer's arrival.

By daylight all of Chisum's natural ugliness lay bared under the harsh light of the summer sun.

Gant had passed a closed-down paint shop on his way along from the jail. Looking around now it was easy to see how an honest paint salesman could go broke swiftly in Chisum. Most of the buildings had never been painted, and those that had were peeling and cracked. There was a long row of uneven holes in the false-front of Parnell's Mercantile, and he studied them for some time before realizing they were bullet holes.

He looked south beyond town to the somber blue face of the Funeral Mountains, Tom Bible's bailiwick. Bible had been rustling cattle in Mescalero County for better than two years, protected by luck, a hardcase crew, the support of Chisum and the natural sanctuary offered by the Funerals. More than once Gant had petitioned Shankland for permission to hunt the rustlers down but it seemed there was always some assignment more immediate and pressing to be taken care of first.

A year earlier the Bible bunch had ambushed a posse here and killed three men including a deputy sheriff.

He wondered if Bible would continue to find Chisum so hospitable after Tucker was hanged.

That thought led to another; what would happen when Tom Bible eventually heard he was back, wearing a star. Might not that hellion see this as a chance to bag himself a marshal and in so doing raise his stocks around Chisum even higher?

He almost hoped he might try. For this was to be his last job as a town-tamer, surely the riskiest job of them all. He would resign at month's end and viewed the opportunity to ram home permanent law and order here in Chisum as a fine and fitting note to go out on.

His smoke finished, he flicked the butt into the street. As he moved out to the edge of the porch he saw the jailhouse door open. Bragg emerged, stretching his arms. Clean-shaven and decked out in his least dirty shirt, the sheriff looked noticeably better than he had last night, yet still didn't look much like a real lawman.

Gant had left the man in charge of the prisoner and felt he'd scared Bragg sufficiently about what might befall him should he fail, to ensure the man would do his job properly. Should there be any attempt to spring Tucker, Gant was certain it would not be made by daylight.

He consulted his heavy fob watch. Ten-twenty. Time to take a turn of the streets before it got too hot.

He stepped down and made his way toward Peach Street. Passers-by refused to meet his gaze. There were, of course, honest folks in Chisum, but even they were convinced that his presence could bring them nothing but trouble.

To find himself walking alone and friendless in a strange town was nothing new to the peacemaker. He'd been doing it for so long in fact that it was going to seem strange when he no longer wore a star, and people he encountered were not afraid to meet his eye.

'Maybe I've been at it too long already,' he mused.

He'd always known there was a limit to just how long even the most dedicated peacemaker like himself could follow this unnatural and dangerous way of life. And yet the idea of quitting also had its uncertain side. He was far from sure that if and when the time came for him to hang up the Buntline Special, that he would have the resources to be able to slip into the role of rancher, businessman or whatever. Sometimes he wondered, that if he did quit, just how long it might take before he no longer felt it necessary to always sit with his back against a wall and facing the doors.

He paused on the corner of Peach and Trail to fire up a fresh cigar and to remind himself, as he did daily, that he must cut down on the tobacco.

He moved on, passing beneath the gallery of the Bear Flag bordello where two tarnished angels stood in their flimsy working gear taking the morning air.

One called something down to him. As he touched fingers to hatbrim and continued on he dimly heard the other girl say;

'That him, Flo? My, but ain't he a fine lookin' feller, no matter what they say about him. Don't exactly look like a killer, does he?'

This didn't faze him. He'd heard it all before. It was like the stiffness in his right leg where that killer's bullet had caught him. You grew accustomed to it and compensated. If you lost something in one direction it was generally possible to make up for it in another. For instance, he believed he was a split-second faster on the clear and draw than before he was shot.

He had elected to take his patrol at this time to dodge the worst of the heat, yet it was already hot, even for the South-west Territory that time of year.

Dust devils danced along the high red ridge on the north-west side of town, hissing and spinning. Timbers that had never known the kiss of paint shimmered in the heat waves that bounced up from the hot, yellow dust before him. He passed by tumbledown houses, a weary-looking stage depot, and a tiny closed-down newspaper office whose façade was riddled with bullet holes.

He walked as far as the river, finished his smoke there, then started back, following a winding back street that led to Trail.

His gaze missed nothing and he had the distinct impression there were far more eyes upon him right now than those of that fat lady in her doorway or the man squatted in the shade of a scrubby tree yonder.

Chisum had a brooding watchful quality this overheated morning, and there appeared to be a scent about the place that was more than just the stink of horse stable or garbage dump. It was the smell of danger and he recognized it as such. He realized it was far too long since a genuine peacemaker had walked these battered streets, and they resented him fiercely – maybe almost as much as he did them and their criminal ways.

Reaching a corner he paused and flicked his cigar butt away and it disappeared in the deep dust as though in water.

Suddenly he was aware of a presence. He twisted around, right hand dropping instinctively to gunbutt. Then he smiled, something few in Sacramento City had ever seen him do.

'Hello, kid.'

He was around eight years old, tow-headed and bare-footed with large blue eyes that studied him warily.

Gant fished in his pockets for a quarter. He held it out but the boy just stared at it.

Gant flipped the coin high and the kid caught it expertly. He tested it with his teeth, a wise practice for anybody, man or child, in larcenous Chisum. Then, grinning a little, he drew closer and fingered his tattered straw hat back from his brow.

'What's your name, boy?'

'Billy Grace. What's yours?'

'I reckon you know.'

'You the marshal?'

'That's right.'

'Are you gonna hang Jimmy Tucker like Pa says?'

Gant's smile faded. 'Guess I am at that. . . .'

'Jimmy always buys me candy when he comes to town. His sister's the prettiest lady I ever saw. Why are you going to hang him? My Pa says Jimmy would never hurt nobody.'

Gant sighed.

'He killed a man, kid. It could have been your father. You can't go round killing people, you know?'

'You do, don't you, mister? Pa says you've killed

more men than the plague.'

The marshal attempted a smile but it didn't come off. 'Better skeedaddle home . . . your ma might be worried.'

The kid turned to go. 'Thanks for the quarter, mister.'

'You're welcome.'

The badgeman's eyes narrowed as he watched the boy scuttle off down the alleyway on bare brown feet. Gant's weaknesses were few but sometimes a child could find them out. There had even been times in the past when he'd thought of settling, getting wedded and raising kids of his own, like Billy Grace. But here he was, thirty-five years of age and half-done with life, and no wife or child of his own. . . .

He shrugged and moved on, walking slowly down the block until he caught sight of a strange-looking edifice looming beyond the rusted roof of an old barn. He halted and frowned at the spidery construction for a long moment before realizing he was staring up at the cross-beam of what could only be a gallows. Casting his mind back, he eventually recalled that Cord Clinton, the last legitimate peace officer they'd had here, was said to have carried out hangings in Chisum before somebody shot him dead with a double blast from a shotgun.

He headed around the corner to take a closer look at their gibbet.

FOUR

GALLOWS CORNER

The fierce red rooster with the mean eye sat atop the gallow's lofty crossbar, peering down at Gant. There was ample visual evidence that the rooster and his flock had been sleeping up there for years.

The marshal crinkled his nose and moved upwind.

A length of clothes line stretched from the upright across the wildly overgrown vacant lot and vanished into the back porch of the decrepit barn. The line was festooned with shirts, underwear, a pair of women's outsized pantaloons and an array of diapers.

From beneath the high veranda and between two of the rickety steps, a pair of eyes studied him fixedly.

'Hey, come out here a minute!' he ordered.

A scruffy urchin in hand-me-downs emerged warily. At the same moment, a vast female emerged from the tumbledown dwelling, and she showed no sign of caution at all.

'Will . . . yum!' she bellowed. 'Will-yum, c'mere away from the nasty man.'

William vanished. The red rooster flapped its wings defiantly, then crowed. Gant scowled as a scruffy man emerged from the old shanty to range up alongside the woman who was twice his size. They appeared ready to attack but he got in first.

'This is the Gallows Corner block shown on the town map at the jailhouse as such, I take it?' he demanded.

'Who wants ter know?' the man demanded.

The fat lady banged his shoulder to silence him, then squinted suspiciously at the star on Gant's vest.

'You're him, ain't yer?' she accused. 'You be the fancy new lawman they's all gabbin' about?'

'That's right,' he replied. 'And all of you are trespassing upon and polluting government property. I'm giving you until dark down to get gone and take this junk heap of a shack with you!'

'Oh gawd, 'Arry,' the large woman gasped in faked fear, realizing up close that the stranger had the look of real trouble now. She slapped brick red cheeks with fat hands. 'This is 'im they warned us about – the new sheriff and 'angman! I thought they was just tryin' to scare us into leavin' our lovely 'ome when they said he would be comin' around. . . .'

She paused a moment to become outraged. 'Oh, what sort of a fiend are you, Mr Marshal? Throw poor innocent folks into the street . . . and even worse, 'ang a lovely boy like poor innocent Jimmy Tucker. Oh, Henry, don't you understand? This is the one that's fixin' to swing that poor innocent boy right 'ere on our chicken roost—'

Gant silenced her with a curt gesture. There may have been a humorous side to this situation but he didn't see it. Life was real and grim from behind a five-pointed star and in his time he'd seen too many communities brought down by disrespect, lack of discipline or worst of all, contempt for the law.

So he stated his orders again then posted himself across the street and somberly watched a totally intimidated fat lady and her squatter clan demolishing their rickety shack for an hour, and only then turned to go.

'I will be back at sundown to see the job is properly completed,' he announced, speaking directly to the man. 'I'm sure it will be.'

Crackley, for that was his name, nodded. He was scared. But not so his lady wife.

'Oh, what sort of a fiend are you, Mr Marshal?' she suddenly erupted. 'How could you take a poor boy like that and just . . . just murder him upon this evil construction like he was just . . . just—'

'Tonight!' Gant rapped, then strode away with Hortense Crackley's curses following him all the way to Trail Street.

He halted upon reaching the main stem to light a cheroot. He glanced back the way he'd come when a mocking voice sounded from the hotel porch close by.

'You've certainly got a knack for making friends, haven't you, Marshal?'

The badgeman stared coldly at the seated figure of Judge Judah Nimrod, before turning on his heel without a word to cross the street. Here his attention was drawn to the stone water trough which still showed several deep old bullet scars. His jaw muscles worked and memories were crowding in on him as he approached the jailhouse.

He halted on sighting the paint pony at the tie-rail. His gaze leapt to the jailhouse door. He mounted the steps and entered so abruptly the young woman seated across the desk from the sheriff turned with a start.

'What's the meaning of this, Mr Bragg?' he demanded. 'I gave specific instructions that you were to admit nobody during my absence.'

Bragg rose. 'I'm sorry, Marshal, but—'

'Never mind the excuses.' He swung upon the girl. 'You will kindly leave, madam. Now.'

She rose uncertainly and Mel Bragg blurted, 'You don't understand, Marshal. This here is Rebecca Tucker. She's young Jimmy's sister.'

Gant removed his hat as the hard street glitter faded slowly from his eyes. His head tilted back a little as he studied her intently.

She was beautiful.

Beauty had never seemed a matter of great

importance to the lawman, but Jimmy Tucker's sister really was a stunner. Tall and slender with a long-legged, high-breasted figure, she was dressed today in open-necked shirt and snug denim riding pants. Her hair was a lighter shade of blonde than her brother's and was worn long, held at the nape of the neck with a crimson bow. An oval face dominated by wide-set dark eyes surveyed the badgeman calmly.

'Miss Tucker,' he said at length, his voice formal and remote.

'Marshal.' She glanced across at the sheriff, then back to Gant. 'I didn't intend to get Sheriff Bragg into trouble, but—'

'No real trouble, Miss Tucker. I simply didn't realize who you were. You wish to visit with your brother, of course?'

The girl's surprise showed. 'You'd allow me to see Jimmy?'

Gant's jaw muscles worked. 'Miss Tucker, we're only the guardians of the law, not brutes bent on inflicting pain and misery, regardless of what you might have been led to believe.'

'Oh, I'm sorry if I conveyed that impression—'

'You wish to see him now?'

'Surely, if I may.'

His eyes ran over her superb figure. 'Miss Tucker, I won't subject you to a physical search. I'm sure you wouldn't attempt anything foolish, yet I feel obliged to warn you that if you did anything foolish I would have no option but either to shoot you down or have you arraigned on capital charges that might well lead to your own execution. Do I make myself clear?'

'Quite clear, Marshal. But to set your mind at rest, I'm not carrying anything more dangerous than a hairpin. May I see my brother now?'

'Certainly.'

She turned and moved down the corridor. Gant followed her thoughtfully then crossed to the wall to hang his hat on a peg.

'Go take a turn of the streets, Mr Bragg.'

'Sure, Marshal.'

'And while you are at it, check out the gallows, will you? I left instructions it was to be cleaned up and returned to its original condition with all trash and squatters removed. I want to know if that has been done.'

'Whatever you say, Marshal.'

When the man was gone Gant lowered himself into a canvas-backed chair and sat facing the cells. Rebecca Tucker stood with her back to him at the door of her brother's cell. They held hands through the bars as they talked.

Those linked hands disturbed the town-tamer as did the girl herself.

She was nothing like he expected and he didn't care for surprises. In truth, neither brother nor sister had proved as anticipated. He'd envisioned Jimmy Tucker as a hatchet-faced young hellion whose eventual end on the gallows would impart a feeling of satisfaction and achievement. It irked him to realize he'd almost come to like this prisoner, and somehow this surprise was only aggravated by his reaction to meeting the sister.

Tucker bore no resemblance to his notorious father, while the sister would have been far better suited to the role of a nurse or possibly a glamorous actress.

The marshal was a hard man accustomed to dealing with hellions and lawbreakers who looked like what they were! The Tuckers offended him with their appearance of quality and – he stumbled on the word – even innocence.

Seated motionless, listening to the soft murmur of voices, he reviewed the Tucker case in his mind.

One week prior to the murder, Jimmy Tucker and hardcase Hec Oliver were alleged to have become involved in a wrangle which eventually led to a brawl. Following the fight, more heated words were exchanged with Oliver taunting Tucker as the son of a killer.

The two had parted with heated words and Oliver was subsequently found dead with a bullet in the back.

A friend of Oliver's claimed Jimmy was responsible and then a rancher neighbor of the Tuckers, Shad Fellows, had visited the sheriff's office at Sweet Creek to inform him that he'd sighted Tucker fleeing the murder scene.

The arrest followed quickly and at the trial, Tucker's main line of defence was that he'd been away on a visit to a strange old hermit named Moses Brown in the Funerals at the time the murder took place. The law had sought to locate this hermit afterwards but found him missing from his usual haunts. Soon after came the trial, damning evidence from Fellows, the guilty verdict and the inevitable death sentence.

Gant never dwelt on a case once the verdict was in. He refused to do so now yet was aware that he frequently found himself musing about rascally Moses Brown.

The old man had on several occasions attempted to persuade him to give up the violent life of the peacemaker, but without success.

He looked up from his thoughts to see the girl he'd been reflecting upon now approaching. Rebecca dabbed at her eyes with a square of lace but slipped the kerchief away as he rose from his chair.

'I wish to thank you, Marshal,' she said quietly, drawing up. 'I-I appreciate the fact that you didn't harm Jimmy when you recaptured him.'

'There was no need, Miss Tucker.'

'He-he told me that he begged you to kill him.'

Gant didn't reply. What could you say to something like that?

'Don't you think it terrible that a boy of Jimmy's age should actually want to die, Marshal Gant?'

'I never think much on such matters.'

She studied him gravely. 'He didn't do it, Marshal. Jimmy didn't kill Hec Oliver.'

'You'd hardly be expected to say anything else, Miss Oliver.'

'But it's true. My brother is innocent.'

'A judge and jury found him guilty.'

'I've had plenty of time to wonder about that. Tell me, Marshal, do you believe it was the evidence against Jimmy that convinced the jury of his guilt . . . or the fact that his father's name happened to be Shep Tucker?'

'You're asking me to speculate. I try never to do that.'

'Then I'll answer for you, Marshal. The prosecuting attorney made many allusions to my father and his record during the trial in Sacramento City. Both judge and jury were given a long, detailed account of your gunfight with my father here in Chisum. Do you think that was fair? They were not trying my brother, Marshal Gant, they were trying my father all over again!'

'The law found him guilty.'

'And the law is never wrong?'

'Rarely.'

'I'm sure you've never been wrong in your life, have you? How wonderful it must be never to have made a mistake.'

Gant stiffened.

'Miss Tucker—' he began stiffly, but broke off when a knock sounded on the door. Hand on gun handle, he moved to the window and looked out. A tall, well-dressed man in a brown suit stood upon the porch. Gant went to the door and jerked it open.

'Yes?' His tone was terse.

'Shad!' the woman exclaimed, moving past Gant. 'What on earth are you doing here in town?' She turned to Gant. 'I'm forgetting my manners. Marshal, this is Mr Shad Fellows. Shad, Marshal Gant.'

'An honor, Marshal,' the man assured, pumping his hand. 'I've heard a lot about you, all of it good.'

Gant nodded gravely and Fellows turned back to the girl.

'I stopped by at the Lazy K to see you, Becky. Tim Bodie told me you'd come to town to visit Jimmy. Naturally that worried me, considering the danger, so I rode in immediately. You really shouldn't be here. Not at this time.'

'Of course I should be,' she defied him. 'My place is with Jimmy now more than ever.'

'You must understand, Marshal,' Fellows weighed in. 'Rebecca and I are very close friends, and I'm concerned for her safety.'

'Well, I reckon your advice is sound,' Gant conceded after a silence. He nodded. 'I believe you'd do well to follow Fellows's advice, Miss Tucker. You'd be aware of the tension my bringing your brother back to Chisum has stirred up . . . so I reckon the best place for you right now would be back home on your ranch.'

'My safety is not my prime concern right now, Marshal Gant,' the girl stated firmly. 'All I'm interested in is my brother, who I can only hope and pray some miracle might save from the gallows.'

Fellows reached for the girl's hand, but Gant noticed she drew back.

'Come on, Becky,' the rancher urged. 'This is no place to talk. Let me buy you coffee and we'll decide on things calmly and sensibly.'

The girl sighed. Of a sudden she appeared totally exhausted. 'Oh, very well, Shad. But you won't change my mind. I'm staying on in Chisum.'

'Well, we'll see,' Fellows said placatingly. 'You'll excuse us, Marshal Gant?'

'Of course.'

Gant stood in the doorway watching the couple walk away along the plankwalk as they made toward the Diamond Spot eatery. He watched until they'd turned into the diner, then closed the door and made his way along the corridor.

He found Jimmy Tucker standing by the window, smoking. He glanced at Gant then returned his bleak gaze to a small strip of blue sky beyond the bars.

'That was Shad Fellows,' Gant said.

'Yeah . . . I know.'

'Good friend of your sister's, I take it?'

Tucker shrugged as though he found the subject of little interest. 'They've been keeping company a spell. Fellows is keen but Sis just puts up with him, I reckon.'

'And he's the man you say lied against you at your trial?'

'Right.'

'So . . . a man who's keeping company with your sister has helped destroy you. That's what you want me to believe?'

'Right now I don't give much of a damn what you believe or not, lawman. But sticking to facts I can tell you Fellows has been trying to buy my spread for a year. The Lazy K joins his Chain Ranch, and the K's got the best water and winter grass anyplace hereabouts. Who knows? Mebbe, when I landed in a fix Fellows simply saw the chance of gettin' rid of me, marryin' Sis, and getting his hands on the K the easy way?'

Gant made to reply but with sudden impatience the other cut him off.

'Look, just leave me be, Marshal. Becky shook me up. I hate like hell her seeing me like this. Just beat it, will you? Go write up your reports or drink whiskey or whatever fellas like you do while they're settin' around waitin' to hang innocent men.'

Gant just nodded and left.

He made his slow way back down the corridor to his office, his expression pensive, his frown deep cut, vaguely conscious of the faint trace of perfume still in the air.

His expression changed suddenly as he realized the first canker of doubt concerning Jimmy Tucker's guilt had just entered his mind.

He considered this pensively for a brief time before backing away from it with a shake of the head.

Don't fall for that one, Gant! You've never met one of that breed, bank robber, cattle thief or two-gun felon who didn't protest to the last that he was as innocent as the sunrise.

Once again strong and resolute he moved to the doorway and stood staring out at the hot yellow blast of high noon. It was only then he realized he'd lighted yet another crooked black cigar.

He scowled. He must start cutting down. Again.

FIVE

BADLANDS MOON

Night in Chisum.

Crossing Trail Street, Marshal Matt Gant entered the Lady Jane Saloon where he ordered a glass of Red River Brandy and sipped it neat. He turned to survey the room which had fallen silent upon his entry. Hard, veiled stares met his own. A pair of buffalo hunters sat in a far corner wrangling over a game of monte, and a girl in a vivid crimson dress plucked idly at a piano with a cigarette dangling from the painted red wound of her mouth.

The Lady Jane was doing good business tonight. There were cowboys in from the outlying spreads scattered along the bar and around the gaming tables. The ranch hands appeared both clean and healthy in contrast to most locals. The Lady Jane was Chisum's best saloon. Here, beneath the one roof, a man could try his luck at keno, faro, chuck-a-luck, monte and all the brands of poker. He could roll dice, buck a roulette wheel or even win serious money at dominoes if he chose.

As was his habit upon entering such places, Gant spent time overlooking the room. Analyzing the look, feel and character of a place was both automatic and professional.

The Lady Jane was noisy by this and growing steadily louder, yet to his trained ear this had just about the right sound to it.

There was none of that subtle undercurrent that might suddenly erupt into explosive violence without warning, no unnatural taut quietness which could well herald actual gunplay.

Drunks might well glower across that smoke-filled room at him, but these weren't about to raise any hell. He could most always scent danger before it erupted. If trouble should explode in the Lady Jane at all tonight he was convinced it was still a way off.

His drink finished, Gant pushed outside through the swinging doors and stood watching the street for a time before making across the street for the jailhouse.

He found the door locked.

Nodding in satisfaction he raised his fist and knocked. Bragg let him in and was about to relock the door when Gant gave him an errand to run.

'Go fetch me some chow from the Diamond Spot,' he ordered.

'Sure, Marshal. Anythin' special?'

'Whatever looks non-poisonous will do.'

'On my way, Marshal.'

He looked in on Tucker and found the prisoner standing by the window. He returned through the archway to the office where he took his seat behind the desk. The chair creaked beneath his weight as he leaned back and pressed thumb and forefinger to his eyes.

He was one weary lawman.

Sleep would be an essential tonight if he expected to be sharp tomorrow. That empty cell across from Tucker's would suit just fine. He could sleep there with one eye open.

Twenty minutes later Bragg returned with a covered tray. He placed it upon the desk before him then whipped away the cloth like a magician performing some spectacular trick.

'*Voilà*! So, what does that look like, Marshal?'

It looked exactly like a double-sized serving of spare ribs, collard greens, chili sauce, hot biscuits and a large slab of corn bread.

'What are you trying to do, Sheriff? Sink me without trace?'

'Thought you looked a mite peaked, Marshal. 'Specially so after Miss Becky stopped by here this mornin'.'

Frowning, Gant sliced off a slab of roast beef. It was delicious. He chewed thoughtfully then grabbed a biscuit. He hadn't realized just how hungry he was.

Bragg hefted a spare chair and toted it to the far side of the room where he could smoke without interfering with Gant's enjoyment of his meal. Gant glanced across at the man several times while eating. He finally spoke.

'Where did it go wrong for you, Mr Bragg?'

'Go wrong, Marshal?'

'You know what I mean. For you to end up masquerading as a lawman in a mean town like this?'

Bragg shrugged.

'Well, mebbe you won't believe it, but I always had genuine respect for the law. But I wasn't in this job here five minutes afore I discovered I never had what it really took to stand up to the genuine hardcases. So I figured I could help out around here and keep things somewhere near the mark without steppin' on too many dangerous toes. Sorta like Nimrod, you know. Enforcing law but not running any personal risks – just like he does.'

'That fraud!'

'He ain't really such a bad feller, Judge Nimrod. Oh, sure, he hits the bottle somethin' fierce, and he could talk a man into hospital. But the man really cares, Marshal. He cares about plain folks and about the law. I like to think that, like me, he does what he can ... or at least what he's allowed to do in a helltown.'

'Fraud!' Gant repeated.

'You don't look kindly on any kind of make-do – do you, Marshal?'

'Never did, never will.'

'Everybody can't be like you, Marshal Gant. We ain't all made of. . . .' His voice faded and he flushed.

Gant speared a potato. 'Go on, Sheriff, say it. Made of rock? Or iron, maybe? You can't dent my feelings. I've been hearing those sort of remarks every day I've spent behind this badge.'

Bragg smiled. 'Well, guess you got to admit you do kinda give the feelin' that you ain't like normal folk . . . Judas! There I go again!'

'Here, have a rib, Mr Bragg. And don't fret about my feelings. But who can tell? If I whip you into shape while I'm here then maybe after I'm gone you'll find yourself able to handle things like a real lawman . . . it's really not that tough.'

The sheriff was smiling now as he crossed the room to pour himself another joe. 'You know, Marshal Gant, it just occurred to me that maybe you ain't as hard and iron-mouthed as you seem at first sight—'

He broke off abruptly and glanced at the barred windows as the sounds of loud shouting were suddenly to be heard heard rolling down the street.

'Hey! What are they yellin' out, Marshal?'

Gant was lunging for the doors when the voices sounded again. There was no mistaking what they were hollering this time as the spine tingling cry of 'Fire!' swept the length of the street.

He reefed the door open and with Bragg close behind, crossed the rickety porch. Flames were

61

leaping into the sky somewhere beyond Parnell's Mercantile and already the dark figures of citizens were to be seen rushing down the street, buckets rattling, shouting.

Gant stood motionless for a moment as realization hit home. The angle they were on plus the position of certain landmarks including the old stage depot, told him clearly where the uproar was coming from.

Gallows Corner.

He swore viciously and his jaw set like a rock as he jerked out the Buntline to check the loads. 'You get back inside and lock the door behind you, Sheriff,' he barked. 'Move!'

The lawman obeyed with alacrity. Gant waited until he heard key turn in lock then jumped down into a rapidly filling street. The height and fury of the flames warned it was likely already too late to save the gallows. But if he was quick enough to grab whoever'd set that fire then he'd rate that a victory.

He was halfway along Trail with men pouring in from the side streets when he stopped on a dime as a thought jolted home. What if this fire had been staged for the purpose of luring him away from the jailhouse – as it had just succeeded in doing?

He shot a look back. With people still rushing by visibility was reduced, yet he felt half-way sure he'd caught a brief flicker of movement down the alleyway flanking the jailhouse building down toward the horse corral in back.

Momentarily indecisive, he looked at the fire

again. By this time, flames were leaping a hundred feet into the air and it was obvious it would be too late to be of any real help down there now.

For another hanging moment he grappled with the reality of the fire as opposed to the uncertainty he felt each time he glanced back at the slate-gray roof of the jailhouse.

Finally, he swore and turned back.

He sprinted to the first cross street then followed it back to the main stem at the run, jostling with citizens making in the opposite direction for the fire. A man crashed into him accidentally. Gant swatted him aside with a six-gun barrel and left him dazed in the dust as he rushed on to find himself soon passing the closed-down paint store and the hardware store. The jailhouse loomed.

His breath was rasping in his throat as he approached the high-railed structure of the law office corrals. Bragg's buckskin, Jimmy Tucker's roan saddler and the Countess were all housed here. One of the animals whickered as he reached the fence in a low crouch, and a split-second later came a hoarse whisper from the open door of the jailhouse;

'We're takin' too much time, goddamnit!'

Then, 'Shut up your gripin'!'

A pause, then, 'What in hell is holdin' you up, Vestry? Ain't you got them hasps worked free yet?'

'Goddamn things are rusted,' panted another voice. 'But . . . but looks like they're givin' finally. . . .'

Swift and silent the marshal snaked around the

63

corral's north side to glimpse a knot of dust-shrouded figures clustered around the jailhouse's rear door. Having already heard Vestry's name, he now caught a fleeting glimpse of Joe Ritchie's curly brown thatch. The third man with the fat behind would have to be Karl Heath, while the *hombre* with bull shoulders could only be rugged Tom Jethro.

'For the love of Pete, we ain't got all mortal night, Vestry!' Jethro complained. 'That trigger-happy son-of-a-bitch tinstar could've smelt somethin' and be halfway back from our fire by this!'

'He's already back!' Gant's voice sounded loud as a gunshot.

Four men whirled as one.

For a handful of seconds the four appeared frozen. Gant thought he had them bluffed before big Jethro bellowed and rushed him. In the background he caught a glimpse of Vestry leaping away to his left with flight plainly uppermost in his mind.

The lawman's right fist exploded in Jethro's face, knocking him off his feet. Instantly Gant lunged to his right, his gun barrel blurred and Vestry was driven into the wall with a vicious red weal across his forehead.

Instantly the lawman spun round and charged the others. The gun barrel flashed with rapier speed and both Heath and Ritchie tumbled off the broad stoop like a pair of tenpins.

With blood streaming from nose and mouth, Tom Jethro somehow struggled to his feet, mouthing

64

obscenities. The heavyweight hurled a vicious blow but Gant swayed lithely from the hips and the whistling fist hissed past his jaw, missing by inches. He countered with a solid left hook that exploded under the ear. As a dazed Jethro slumped to ground a vicious chop across the back of the neck caused his eyes to roll in their sockets – out to the world.

Matt Gant was standing calmly fingering back his hat by the time the frightened voice sounded through the jailhouse door.

'W-what's goin' on out there?'

'It's all right, Mr Bragg, this is the marshal. Open up!'

There was the sound of a heavy draw-bolt being pulled back. Then Sheriff Bragg appeared warily. Gant noted with approval that the man had his old-fashioned Dragoon model Colt clasped in a shaky fist. Bragg gaped bug-eyed at the sprawled figures then focused upon the town-tamer.

'What in Hades is goin' on here, Marshal?'

'It's called law enforcement. You can put that weapon away now and help me haul these gentlemen into the cells.'

SIX

CAME A WILD STRANGER

Clancy, the Gallows Corner tramp was having his worst ever night. It had begun badly when he'd been hunted from his customary lair in back of the gallows by several heavy blows from Hortense Crackley's big broom. He'd shared the overgrown lot with the Crackleys through its years of misuse, but Hortense always treated him badly. He'd been forced to sulk for hours in the hovel across the street while the chastened Crackley clan revamped the gallows with brushes, mops and brooms until it hardly looked like the old home any more.

But that was only the beginning. Pocketing his pride, and deeply resentful of the spick-and-span unfamiliarity of his former hideaway in the heart of town, the raggedy old bum had just stealthily moved back when some fool came creeping up through the high weeds to splash coal oil over the gallows base. The sudden flare of a vesta and leap of flames had sent Clancy scooting back across the street from which point he watched the old home go up in smoke while deputies officiously shifted the Crackley clan out to an abandoned woolshed on the south side of town – permanently.

Despite the crowd that gathered to watch the holocaust, Clancy managed to drop off again, didn't awaken for several hours until aroused by the sounds of industry. The area was now lit by burning brands and some half-dozen town tradesmen were hard at work with hammers and saws working on the gallows repairs and supervised by a formidable figure in dark garb with a five pointed star pinned to his lapel.

The working party maintained its feverish pace throughout the day, and come dusk Clancy and a large number of citizens were gathered at the corner admiring Chisum's brand new gallows.

Clancy listened to all the talk about how a new marshal and a new gibbet were sure signs that Chisum was finally emerging from its dark age of wild men and lawlessness with a bright new future just around the corner.

Clancy knew different. That overgrown lot had been his home and refuge for years and would soon be so again. He'd seen lawmen come and go, although none as formidably impressive as the current Marshal Gant, it was true. But one by one they had been killed or driven out and he was confident the current occupant of the jailhouse would prove no exception. Gant would go, the Crackleys were already gone, and in time Gallows Corner would be his safe haven once more.

There were just two things capable of putting hangman Milton Gotham off his food – travel and excitement.

On this morning the Territorial executioner had hanged badman Judah Henry and was now en route to the town of Chisum where he was scheduled to exercise his grim profession yet again, and as a consequence was unable to do full justice to the fare at Parsley's Way Station.

So, settling with what was for him just a snack of eight flapjacks drenched in maple syrup along with rashers of prime bacon fried in butter washed down with three mugs of extra-strength coffee, the executioner pushed himself back from the table, got up and paid his check.

His covered buggy stood harnessed and waiting when he emerged from the station, squinting against the hot yellow glare of the early sun. The station hostler, who had just been informed of the identity of their solitary guest, tossed him the reins then headed for the sanctuary of the stables at a hasty walk-trot.

There were few citizens anyplace who ever wanted to be seen socializing with a hangman.

Gotham paid no attention to the hostler's attitude. He was accustomed to this sort of reaction wherever he went, and he constantly travelled far and wide in a profession where there was always work available for a solid reliable hangman. The buggy springs creaked beneath his ponderous poundage as he lowered his shiny black pants onto the leather seat. He grabbed up the reins and released the brake, his movements smooth and sure. The horse responded to the slap of reins and soon the county hangman was swinging away down the trail, shiny yellow buggy wheels glinting in the sunlight.

The Territorial executioner weighed in at just over three hundred pounds and measured one hundred twenty-five inches around the girth. His mountainous bulk was encased in shiny black broadcloth and he wore an enormous white hat for protection against the sun. Between fat cheeks flushed by excess, a fleshy nose dominated a small pink mouth. His eyes held the bright, beady intensity of a packrat.

There was something grossly comical about the hangman – at first glance. But up close the veteran of so many executions in wild South-west Territory projected a commanding and sinister quality which invariably silenced the flippant remark or smirking jest. Heavy-belly Gotham they called him back in his hometown, but never to his face.

As was always the case, Gotham was eagerly looking forward to his next assignment. Apart from his fifty-dollar fee, the fat man derived great pleasure from his trade. He had nothing but contempt for those who would show mercy to vicious criminals. His tidy mind appreciated the sense of justice and total finality that went with a good execution.

In the case of wild Jimmy Tucker, the man had been found guilty of murder as a matter of course. It had been a straightforward sort of killing as murders went. But Gotham was very much aware that Jimmy Tucker was the son of infamous Shep Tucker, and he was looking forward keenly to this assignment for the opportunity it would provide to show the entire Territory that murder would always reap its just reward, regardless of the condemned's connections.

Gotham was already convinced that the execution of someone of Tucker's notoriety would set the seal on his reputation as the Territory's best at his trade, the crowning feather in his ambitious cap.

He licked pudgy lips with a plump pink tongue. Days like this it was great to be alive and it was just too bad that handsome young Jimmy Tucker would be unable to share his enjoyment of it.

The gunman arrived just on dusk, walking his tall palomino horse by the shadowed porch of the Lady Jane Saloon where a group of loafers sat watching him with sudden interest.

They saw a lean six-footer with a cruel hawk face and long black hair. He was flashily dressed in ornate calf boots, richly flowered vest, low-crowned dark hat and double shell belt.

The newcomer flashed a grin at the loungers, the teeth very white against the deep tan of his face. There was about this one a hint of wildness, as though he might have just ridden across a hundred unmapped miles with his long hair blowing and that big flashy cayuse flying before a prairie wind. Man and horse both looked wild, even by Chisum standards.

The newcomer checked in at the Chuckwagon Hotel and signed his name with long nimble fingers that might have graced the hand of an artist or concert pianist. But although Harley Raingo was an artist of sorts, his was an art exemplified by the big white-handled guns that he carried slung butt-forward and buckled to lean thighs.

His name was well-known in Chisum and the town was buzzing with the talk of his arrival some thirty minutes later when he strolled into the Lady Jane to pinch a percentage girl's plump bottom and order a large rye whiskey.

The barkeep was still making change for the gunman's dollar when the batwings swung inwards and Gant stood in the doorway with the Territory night forming a black background behind him.

The eyes of lawman and badman met and locked. Then Gant came halfway along the bar to halt ten feet from Chisum's new arrival.

'What brings you here, Raingo?'

The white smile flashed. 'Now, is that any way to greet an old pard, Marshal? Come on, let me buy you

71

a shot for old time's sake—'

'I said – what are you doing here?'

The smile faded, as any smile would in the face of such a chilly welcome.

'Just drifted in, Gant,' Raingo said quietly. 'Why?'

'That's a lie.'

The room hushed at the words for Harley Raingo was a man with a deadly reputation. But if the onlookers expected the man to take offence or go for iron, they were mistaken.

The gunman allowed a long moment's silence to drift by before he spoke. 'You sure ain't changed any, have you, Gant?'

'Marshal Gant to you. And no, I haven't changed at all. I'm still the same man who called your bluff in Arizona, then beat the stuffing out of you.'

Slowly and deliberately Harley Raingo raised his right hand and dragged the back of it across his mouth, dark eyes smoldering. Yet his tone remained mild when he spoke.

'I remember that day real good.'

'You should. For that was the luckiest day you ever lived. Had you gone for iron, I'd have killed you. Or if you'd been wanted in the Territory at that time I'd have brought you back and seen you hanged.'

The silence seemed to thicken. The lawman moved closer to stand squarely before this man in the flowered vest and fancy boots.

'So, you won't tell me why you're here?'

'Just told you.'

'All right, I'll make an educated guess, Raingo. You heard I was here and why. You also heard I'd be alone without any real backing in a hostile town. So, you figured that if you were to drift in you just might get a chance to even some old scores.'

'You're talkin' loco, Gant. I wouldn't—'

'I'm still talking. Okay, I'll admit I can't legally boot your fancy backside out of town, because this is still a free country even for gunsharks like you. But hear this. You make one wrong move, pilgrim – just one – and I'll come after you. Knowing you, that'd likely lead to gunplay, and I'm faster than you. So you'd wind up dead and I'd still be walking the streets wearing this star. Is that how you see things unfolding if you stick around?'

The saloon by this time was totally still. Harley Raingo stood motionless with hot color in his cheekbones, dark eyes smoldering deep in their sockets.

Seconds dragged by on leaden feet before Matt Gant turned his back on the wild man and shouldered his way out through the batwings.

It felt cold upon the porch.

He halted by the railing to take out a cigar, ignoring the porch sitters who'd crowded in close to listen and watch. His hands were steady as he put a match to his tobacco, then drew deeply.

Raingo!

This was something he could have done without. There was ample danger in this meanest of mean

73

towns without adding to it at this late stage.

He felt that in the wake of the amateurish attempted jailbreak the night before he had imposed his authority over the town. But Raingo's appearance was a reminder that in any place like this you could never be sure. It followed that tension would automatically increase as execution day drew closer. Added to that, Bragg had heard a whisper that notorious rustler Tom Bible had announced his intention to show up before the big day.

Well, he'd never reckoned this job would prove easy.

He turned away from the lights and made his slow deliberate way along the walk. Men lounged in groups along the central block, leaning idly against store fronts, or seated upon the tie rails where their horses were tethered. They spoke quietly, and here and there was the quick orange spurt of a match flame. They fell silent as he passed and Gant stared straight ahead.

The marshal sat alone in the gloom of the jailhouse porch. It was almost eleven. Gant had sent Bragg home to rest up at sundown in order that the man could stand watch later while he grabbed some shut-eye.

Night owls were still abroad, but beginning to thin out by this. It was growing quiet although there was the occasional yelling and cussing spilling from the Bear Flag.

Gant sat smoking, his hat on a peg before him.

The night had turned cool and the air for once was free of dust. A quarter-moon rode the high sky, casting dappled shadows through the cottonwoods in front of the hardware store.

A woman leading a horse and walking beside a man, appeared around the corner of the Chuckwagon Hotel. The marshal glanced their way idly at first then realized the woman was Rebecca Tucker. He frowned as he watched the man halt and mount up, wave goodbye and ride off. The girl made for the front doors of the hotel before she glanced across at the jailhouse. She hesitated momentarily, then turned and started across.

Gant realized he was brushing his hair back with both hands before he caught himself. What in hell did he think he was doing? It wouldn't matter a rat's to Rebecca Tucker if he was the handsomest *hombre* in the Territory. She would still see him only as the man who would kill her brother.

He rose as she reached the steps. 'Evening, Miss Tucker.'

'Good evening, Marshal Gant. Please don't get up.'

'Have you come to see your brother?'

'No . . . not at the moment. I thought I might talk to you.'

He nodded gravely. He was surprised by just how keenly he wanted to talk with her, even though he didn't expect that to go well. He nodded gravely and gestured at the rocking chair, and she climbed up onto the porch and sat. Resuming his seat, Gant set the cigar between his teeth again while studying her clean, youthful profile in the half light. Daughter of a killer, sister of a killer. This was a reality he found difficult to swallow whenever he found himself in her company.

'How is Jimmy?' she asked at length.

'As well as can be expected.'

'Do you still have Tim Vestry and the others locked up?'

'No.'

'That surprises me, Marshal.'

He shrugged. 'Foolish boys. They canceled out their fines by rebuilding the. . . .' His voice faded.

'The gallows, you mean?'

'Yes.'

'You know why they attempted to free Jimmy, I'm sure, Marshal. Not because they're criminals but because they believe him to be innocent.'

'I could have handed them a year's jail apiece for their actions.' Gant exhaled a cloud of blue smoke, then said abruptly, 'Who was that fellow with you on the street, Miss Tucker? I'm not prying into your personal life, but it's my duty to investigate anybody who might pose a threat to my safety.'

Rebecca leaned back in her chair, linked hands around her knee.

'You need not worry, Marshal. No . . . I'm not cooking up any wild schemes to free my brother. At least, not illegally. The man you saw was Tim Brodie,

76

our hired hand from the ranch. He came in to see me, and I've sent him into the Funerals to make one last attempt to find Moses Brown.'

'You still believe your brother's alibi, then?'

'Of course.'

'Then, what about Fellows's testimony?'

'I know Shad lied.'

'Yet you still see the man?'

'For one reason only, Marshal. The hope that Shad might let something slip and reveal he was lying. Unfortunately, he hasn't done so – yet.' She paused. 'I believe you had some trouble earlier tonight?'

'Raingo, you mean? No trouble really. I have the edge on that gun and we both know it.'

'I sighted him at the hotel some time back. He frightened me. He reminded me of . . . well, that's not important. Is he really the killer they say he is?'

'Indeed he is. But he's a backshooter more than a gunfighter, the lowest breed there is. Raingo simply loves to kill.'

The girl shuddered. 'How could any man enjoy taking a human life?'

That was a question Matt Gant could not answer. He'd killed men in his time and the last had been as hard as the first for him no matter what people might think to the contrary. In truth, it was killing that had in the end brought him to the decision to quit the law after this assignment. He had made a vow that once he handed in the badge he would never draw his gun again as long as he lived.

His leg was cramping. It did this sometimes if he sat for any length of time. He straightened the limb and massaged his thigh absently, then glanced up to see her studying him.

'Does your leg trouble you?'

'Scarce at all.'

'I suppose you don't care to talk about it. Or, at least, not to me.'

'You didn't shoot me, Miss Tucker.'

'But my father did.'

He made no response. He set the cigar between his teeth. When he realized it had gone out he flicked it away.

She said, 'I'm sorry for what my father did to you.'

He shrugged. 'I was trying to kill him. He had the right to defend himself.'

Rebecca grimaced. 'Defend himself? That must have been about the first time he'd ever had to do that. Mostly my father attacked, Marshal, as you would probably know. Attack anybody, everybody. . . .'

He was surprised by her bitterness.

'I never expected to hear you speak like that.'

'Why not?'

'Well . . . he was your father.'

'He was a monster.'

Gant blinked. The chair creaked beneath his weight as he leaned forward. 'What. . . ?'

'I said my father was a monster. Does that surprise you?'

'Some. I guess I assumed that. . . .'

'That simply because he was our father, Jimmy and I should be loyal to him? We hated him. He beat us as children, was cruel to us growing up . . . and my happiest day was when he died.' She grimaced. 'You appear shocked.'

He was. He'd naturally assumed that Jimmy Tucker would have regarded his violent parent as some kind of hero. But the girl's outburst demolished that supposition.

'But Jimmy is totally different from my father,' she hastened to explain. 'He's always been gentle and protective and—'

She stopped at the sound of steps and both turned to see the gangling figure of Bragg approaching. Gant welcomed the diversion for Rebecca Tucker had been touching on things he really didn't want to hear. The three chatted quietly for several minutes before Bragg went inside, and Gant rose, offering to escort Rebecca to her hotel.

She accepted.

The lawman was conscious of odd emotions as they started across Trail. How long was it since he'd had the time or the opportunity to walk with an attractive woman beneath the moon? How long was it since he'd been as acutely conscious of a girl's loveliness as he was then? Too long, was the answer to the former – and never to the latter.

She was just the sort of woman a man could build his dreams around. But he was going to hang her brother.

They reached the porch where she turned to him, something about her eyes suggesting that she sensed what he might be thinking. Gant stood before her, tall and straight yet gripped by an unfamiliar awkwardness. He was searching for the words he wanted when the muffled crash of a shot breached the night's hush.

'Marshal, what—?'

That was all he heard as he spun away to make swiftly towards the sound of screaming that was spilling out from the Bear Flag bordello.

SEVEN

BREAKOUT

Above the clamor spilling from the Bear Flag, Gant suddenly detected the sound of drumming hoofs. Gun in hand, he paused on the Peach Street corner a moment to listen to the fading sounds of the horse, then hurried on.

The moment the mob – which had quickly gathered in front of the bordello – saw him coming, it parted and he strode directly through the opening and into the parlor. Several of the girls were hysterical and he sighted the madam, Kate Grigson, bending over a bloody-shirted man stretched out upon a divan in the corner.

'What happened here?' he demanded.

Everybody began speaking at once. Kate Grigson silenced them with a sharp shout, then came forward.

'There was an argument, Marshal Gant. Hank Piano, over there, and Harley Raingo were—'

'Raingo?' Gant interrupted. 'He shot this man?'

'Yes, indeed, Marshal. It really wasn't the other man's fault. They got to arguing about one of the girls and—'

'Was that Raingo I sighted riding off?' he rapped.

'Yeah, Marshal,' affirmed Brawn Carter. 'I told Raingo to wait up until you showed, but he figured you'd nail him for sure, whether he happened to be in the right or wrong.'

'And he was right,' Gant shot back. 'Carter, you go fetch my horse from the jailhouse.' He motioned with the gun. 'Well, move, dammit – move!'

Carter left at a trot and Kate Grigson had the floor again. 'You plan on going after that man, Marshal?'

Gant had moved away to stand over the bloodied Hank Piano. The man had stopped one in the shoulder. He was leaking plenty blood, but would survive.

'That's so, Miss Grigson.'

'But, Marshal, it was a fair fight. He—'

'A gunslinger against a wood-carter?' he interrupted. 'Fair maybe in your eyes but not in mine, madam. But make no mistake. The letter of the law will be strictly observed. Both these men are guilty of the crime of discharging a firearm in a public place. That is a felony in the statute books. I will arrest Raingo and so charge him. Piano will be similarly dealt with, if he recovers.'

Nobody challenged him. The marshal sounded too sure of his law. And was. But the reality was, Gant would not have spared a moment's concern over the incident had Raingo not been involved. This was a chance he would not pass up. If he succeeded in running Raingo down, then he could arrest him, have him jailed then arraigned before Judge Nimrod in the morning and see to it that the man fetched a minimum five days.

That would keep that troublemaker safely in the cells until after the hanging.

By the time Brawn Carter returned astride Countess, Gant had seen Piano toted away to the medic's and had just sent Judge Nimrod off to the jailhouse to inform Bragg he might be absent several hours. He was surprised when Nimrod had offered to stand watch on Bragg; it seemed a night for surprises.

He mounted immediately and swung off for the south side of town. Less than ten minutes had elapsed since the shot had jolted Chisum's night, and the dust of Raingo's exit still hung in the motionless air above the south trail.

With the town quickly falling away behind him, Gant leaned low over the mare's neck and talked into her ear, urging her on.

Countess responded. Her flowing stride lengthened and the dusty yellow trail flashed beneath flying hoofs. Gant glanced back to see the lights fading fast behind. Then he turned again to the trail ahead and didn't look back, the mare's long mane streaming past his face.

Midnight tolled over the rooftops of Chisum. From the front office, Jimmy Tucker heard the clink of a bottle neck against a glass, then the murmur of Nimrod's voice and Bragg's dry tones in reply.

The town was quiet again following the shooting at the Bear Flag. The slim boy standing smoking by his barred window could hear nothing but the murmur of voices from the office, the faint throb of a distant guitar, the unsteady steps of a drunken towner weaving his way home.

The prisoner sighed and dragged hungrily on his cigarette. After learning Gant had gone off after Harley Raingo, he'd briefly hoped they might come along to the jail and try to spring him. But with two hours already gone, he was slowly coming to realize the truth of the situation. Vestry and the boys had had a bellyfull of jailbreaking, and added to that, Gant had the whole town afraid by this.

Nobody was coming to help him.

Time dragged.

His smoke finished, Jimmy leaned his slim back against the wall and stared at his narrow bunk. He might as well try grab some sleep and run the risk of more of those damned dreams. Dreams of giant nooses, booming trapdoors under his feet and the stony face of a lawman watching him kick his life away on the end of a yellow rope.

He took a step toward the bunk, suddenly propped. He'd clearly heard the sound of a walking horse.

He returned swiftly to the window and peered out. At first he saw nothing. But moving to one side in order to get an angled view of the corral, he glimpsed his roan saddler standing outside the fence.

Astonished, Tucker extended his arm through the bars and clicked his fingers. The horse came to him immediately, stretching up to reach his hand and licking it.

'Now . . . how the hell. . . ?' Jimmy puzzled. Then, pressing his face against the bars, he squinted towards the corral and saw the gate standing open. He'd heard the racket earlier when Brawn Carter had come charging around to to get Gant's fancy black mare. Plainly, in his haste, Carter must have failed to latch that gate properly.

His mind raced as he stared down at the animal, then back to the bars again. The bars were solid and well set, and he'd already tested them out to realize they were too strong for any man to hope to shift.

Yet now with his heart beginning to thud like a triphammer against his ribs, he was reminding himself again and again that a horse was many times stronger than any man. . . .

He swung from the window, eyes scanning the confines of his cell room. Who cared if what was racing through his mind was an impossible long shot or not? It was still worth a try. With his horse loose in the jailhouse yard, surely he could figure how he might make use of such an advantage. . . .

He needed a rope!

Instantly his gaze dropped to his bunk with its tough canvas ticking. Canvas like that, cut into strips and knotted together end-to-end could be fashioned into a sturdy rope. . . .

He snatched up the canvas, tested it with his hands, cursed. Sure, it was sturdy enough for any purpose. But it was too strong, and naturally he didn't have a knife or anything that might be used to cut with.

Desperately he searched the cell looking for something he might employ as a knife. He knew there'd be nothing, which was exactly what he found. He could feel the tension in the big bundle of nerves in his belly tightening up. He began massaging his mid-section to ease the discomfort and realized his fingers were feeling the cold, metallic touch of his outsized steel belt-buckle.

The buckle!

Instantly he stripped off the belt and detached the sturdy steel buckle. He dropped to his knees and within desperate minutes was sweating like a mule skinner from the exertion of rubbing one edge of the buckle against the hard stone floor.

The buckle was growing hot but it was also wearing down along the edges as he continued to force it to and fro against the stone . . . to and fro . . . until the sweat was blinding him and he was afraid his grunting and groaning from the effort must carry through to the front office. . . .

It was the intense work of twenty minutes to grind down one side of the buckle to a knife-blade sharpness by honing it relentlessly against the stone floor.

He was excited but exhausted, but dared not waste a moment as he turned his attention to the canvas sheeting.

He'd already determined the canvas was about as sturdy as canvas could get. This strength would make it ideal for what he had in mind, but was going to make the most important step – the slicing – that much more difficult.

He spread the canvas upon the floor and ran his improvised cutting tool along its length. It cut like a knife! He was grinning hugely, with sweat running down his face, when he heard a chair scrape followed by the sound of slow booted steps.

He barely had time to rearrange his bed and fall upon it, feigning sleep, before the burly figure of Bragg showed at the barred doors.

'Sleepin', kid? You ain't foolin' me none. With that judge and them gallows both waitin' their chance at you right now, you ain't gonna doze worth a cuss afore this and then and we both know it. Right?'

The motionless figure grunted then snored and soon the turnkey shrugged and went back to his comfortable padded chair; he was barely seated before his prisoner was back at work on the cell floor, belt-buckle blade slicing the sturdy canvas like hog fat cheese.

Within ten minutes he had six strips of the tough fabric. Hunkering down, he started in plaiting. He fashioned two seven-foot-long pieces, each comprising three entwined strips, then knotted them together at either end. He finally stood, sweating and holding a fourteen-foot-length of powerful rope in his hands.

His heart leapt at the sound of a voice.

'Hey, you movin' about, kid?' the jailer hollered. 'Want some joe?'

'Leave me be, Bragg, just leave me be!'

'Whatever you say, boy!'

Cold sweat trickled down his flanks as he stood listening to the sounds coming from the front office that told him how long it took the turnkey to brew up, the sounds the man made getting some biscuits out of a tin, at last the grunt and creak of leather as he sat and raised his boots to the desk top.

Tucker moved fast.

Snatching up the rope, he fashioned a strong loop at one end. Then he went to the barred window and fastened the free end securely to the middle bar in the solid-framed, three-bar cell window.

'Hoss!' he hissed.

The horse appeared and Jimmy reached through the bars to seize hold of the mane, then slipped the noose over the big head. The animal shook its head in disgust, then pricked its ears when he heard its own name.

'Go boy!' he whispered urgently. 'Go!'

This was an order he'd taught the animal to respond to instantly whenever he wanted it to break into a gallop. It could not run here but did instinctively rear backwards. Instantly the improvised rope snapped taut and there was a tearing, groaning sound followed by the splintering of breaking cement and brick . . . and slowly but surely the solid-framed, three-barred iron window began to pull loose and slide as the horse backed up in alarm.

With both hands locked around iron bars, Jimmy Tucker allowed himself to be hauled up bodily off the cell floor, ducking low as first his extended arms then his torso were hauled up and through the two feet by three feet empty window space as the frightened horse continued to pull backwards.

Then, with teeth clenched and busted chunks of rubble raking his ribs, his entire upper body burst loose on the free side of the cell wall. He kicked once and he was falling, releasing his grip on his canvas rope and tucking his knees up under his belly as he plummeted down to land – more by luck than design – feet first in the deep grass beneath the window, on the outside of the jailhouse!

Rolling violently and kicking to his feet, he knew he'd never moved faster. A desperate handful of seconds saw him calm the startled horse, rip his canvas rope loose of the head harness then leap high to claw his way astride the animal ... while from within the jailhouse came the sounds of wild cursing, shouts of alarm and tumbling furniture as the marshal's night staff of two fumbled with their door locks in their desperation to see what in hell was happening to their hitherto indestructible jailhouse.

The horse hit the ground running and Tucker was leaning low over the animal's neck as it went storming headlong across the main street of town, scattering walkers and causing a pair of work mules drawing a hay wagon to break into a panicking gallop that saw them demolish a hay stall opposite the law office before vanishing in the direction of the river.

Man and horse went rocketing past the corral and they had been swallowed by the side street before the jailers could get their security door swinging open. Tucker could hear them cursing and shouting as he swept to Frontier Street and stormed along its length before bursting into Trail where man and horse were engulfed in the gloom of evening.

Instantly he cut the wild-eyed horse back to a trot, swung it around and deliberately made his way back along unlit Federal Street toward the hotel. Nobody sighting him in the half-light would associate such a slumped, slow-moving rider with the uproar that had just exploded at the jailhouse.

The ploy worked and he no longer felt he was in immediate danger as he turned into the hotel yard and sighted Mick Mulrooney's curious head poking from an upstairs window. This was a town where young Jimmy Tucker had virtually all friends and no enemies, and he didn't hesitate to halt in a patch of light where Mulrooney could identify him.

'Mick!' he called softly. 'Go rouse Becky, will you. Tell her to get down here at the double!'

Mulrooney's eyes bugged. 'Jimmy?' he marvelled. 'Glory, it *is* you, boy. I'm on my way, kid!'

Swinging away, Tucker heeled the roan to the stable door, jumped down and hurried inside. He had his sister's horse saddled and ready to ride by the time Rebecca came rushing through the rear door.

'Jimmy!' She couldn't believe her eyes. 'How—'

'No time, Sis,' he said urgently. 'Just get up and ride!'

Together they swung up and headed out of the yard.

'Good luck, Jimmy boy,' Mick Mulrooney called softly after them. Then, erasing a smirk, he trotted around the hotel corner and threaded his way across the noisy street to where a stunned Mel Bragg and a white-faced Judge Nimrod stood gazing round in perplexity at all the furious activity. 'Goddammit,' he yelled, 'what's all the hullaballoo about?'

Matt Gant stood under the light of a fading moon staring across the muddy brown waters of the Buffalo River. A short distance upstream, the tracks of Harley Raingo's horse led into the water but didn't show him emerging on the other side.

His intense gaze followed the course of the river

eastward. He'd already soaked himself to the skin while examining the bed of the shallow stream on hands and knees until at last locating the imprints of the horse heading east.

Swinging cold arms for circulation, he concentrated on what he knew and what he reckoned he could guess. There was little doubt in his mind that he could still track Raingo down if he chose, but now knew he must consider the time factor. His watch told him it was after two in the morning. He'd been absent from Chisum for nigh on four hours. That was a long time to be away from town and jailhouse, maybe too long.

Even so, the final decision to quit and head back was hard to make. By nature he hated to start something and leave it unfinished whether it be a simple report to head office or the pursuit of a dangerous fugitive. He wanted Harley Raingo stashed away in a solid cell in order that he'd have one less problem to worry about. Nonetheless, plain instinct warned that he didn't dare stay away from Chisum too long. It was that simple.

Countess whickered softly when he returned. Gant stood stroking her soft velvet muzzle for some minutes. Then, with a sigh, he swung up and waded his way back across the Buffalo.

It was a long ride back.

The moment the marshal identified the distant figure of the rider coming towards him along this sweep of the south trail from Chisum, he sensed the worst. For surely only the worst of all scenarios could force Bragg to come out here when he might be sitting snug inside the locked jailhouse, idly keeping a watchful eye on Jimmy Tucker.

Gant's expression was grim as he booted the black mare into a run to narrow the gap swiftly. Bragg greeted him with a half-wave, then dropped his hand sheepishly. He checked his buckskin saddle horse as the marshal reined in alongside.

'Er, howdy there, Marshal,' he said awkwardly. 'Lucky I caught up with you—'

'What happened?'

Bragg swallowed. 'He-he got away, Marshal. Er – skeedaddled.'

The impact of Gant's stony stare hit the burly badgeman with the impact of a physical push. The lawman's jaw muscles knotted, and when he finally spoke, it was through clenched teeth.

'How?'

Weakly, apologetically, Bragg related the story of the crashout. He still was uncertain how Tucker had swung it. Yet he'd discovered the knotted canvas rope still tied solidly to the ripped-out window frame outside, and he figured out the role the horse must have played. Naturally he'd already searched all over, but the kid was surely gone. And his sister, too.

'Rebecca too?' Gant repeated slowly, stonily. 'Then . . . she must have assisted in the escape.'

Bragg hung his head. 'I, er, reckon not, Marshal.

93

You see, after Jimmy busted his way loose . . . well . . . I guess he kinda rode around to the hotel and, like, collected her.'

'Did he happen to stop off for coffee and crackers as well?'

The marshal's tone was sarcastic, bitter.

'I'm right sorry, Marshal. But I simply never figured he'd have the nerve to try somethin' like that. I was plenty confused, let me tell you, and the judge wasn't much help and. . . .' His voice trailed away.

Anger was an ashy taste in Gant's mouth. Yet his anger had already shifted from Bragg and switched back to himself for leaving the man with a responsibility he simply was not equipped to handle. Yet even with the concession made, it still cost him some effort to say what came next.

'It's all right, Mr Bragg. What's done is done.'

The sheriff brightened immediately. 'That is mighty white of you to say so, Marshal.'

Gant didn't even hear. He was thinking hard now, assessing, guessing, trying to think like a man on the run. After a minute, he said, 'Do have have any notion which way they went?' He might have added, 'After they completed a tour of the town.' But didn't.

'Reckon so, Marshal. After I found out about the sister and all, I mounted up and started trackin' some. I saw where they rode out north a couple of miles, then begin to swing away to the south. I figured they must be heading back to the Lazy K or, even more likely, for the Funerals beyond their spread. I rode back in and called for a posse, but that was like droppin' your bucket down a dry well. No takers. Then I figured the next best thing was to come lookin' for you. I knew you'd rode the south trail so I—'

'Just a minute. How far would it be from here to the Lazy K?'

'Why, about twenty miles as the crow flies across that range yonder, Marshal. For anybody but a crow it'd be closer to thirty miles or more. But if you're thinkin' of goin' out after 'em, sir, they got too much head start. They'll be lickin' right along as fast as they can skeedaddle, of that you can be sure. You wouldn't—'

'You said as the crow flies, Mr Bragg,' Gant cut in, staring south-east at the rugged range which spurred up from the Funerals far out across the plains. 'You mean over that range?'

'The Catamounts? Yeah, them's what I mean, Marshal. But you couldn't—'

'Is it possible to ride across that range?'

'Why, I suppose it'd be possible, if a man wanted to risk—'

'But it's possible that the Tuckers might have taken that route, then?'

'Marshal, that ride would just about flatten the toughest man. A female gal simply wouldn't make it.'

The man's words had the ring of good sense. And yet the marshal was aware of a faint pulse of hope as he considered. It seemed probable that Johnny and Rebecca Tucker had, as Bragg suggested, elected to ride either for the ranch or the mountains beyond.

Experience had taught the lawman that a fugitive would almost invariably make for familiar terrain in flight. The Tuckers would know he'd come after them, and, knowing that, they'd require supplies and possibly fresh horses to see them through.

There was no way they'd be wasting one second. But would they ride all out? They would know Bragg would be unable to muster a posse or give chase, and they would reason that they wouldn't have to worry about himself, the marshal, until he'd returned from the chase after Harley Raingo. They might feel they had time to make that rugged crossing, and once they had it behind them there was a thousand miles of open country they could vanish into down south. . . .

He was thinking fast now. Was it possible that if he were to drive directly across the Catamount Hills he might still stand an outside chance of catching them before they quit the ranch? And even should they bypass the spread, there might still be a good chance of cutting their sign and tracking them into the high country.

Gant looked noticeably less grim than he had done as he turned back to the sheriff now. 'Mr Bragg, if I were to ride across the Catamounts, what route would bring me out of there near to the Lazy K?'

Bragg pointed.

'See that white cliff face about due south, Marshal, just under that twisted bluff? Well, that there is the way you'd go. There's an old line-rider's trail up there someplace, but it sure is powerful steep and I still reckon you shouldn't—'

'I'm sure there's good horse sense in everything you say, Mr Bragg. Now, would you oblige me by stepping down?'

Bragg blinked. 'You mean you want my horse?'

'Indeed I do.'

'But, Marshal, it's nigh ten miles back to town.'

'Haven't you heard, Mr Bragg? Walking is considered the finest tonic for the sluggish liver.' His grin vanished and his tone turned sharp. 'Come on, don't shilly-shally, man, I've a fugitive to run down. You can walk to the nearest spread and borrow a horse to ride back and the office will foot the bill. Move, man!'

It was a reluctant Mel Bragg who slid to the ground and silently passed Gant the lines. The marshal grunted then swung around in a horse length and heeled away swiftly across the plains for the Catamount Hills.

Bragg watched the receding figures of man and horses for a time before turning to stare south. The nearest spread? That was the Double Eagle, at least five miles distant. He hadn't walked that far since he'd been in short pants.

With a massive sigh, the lawman started off. It wasn't even full sunup yet but the morning was already hot. Bragg reckoned the temperature would be well past the century mark by the time he reached the Double Eagle.

'You play the game hard, Marshal,' he complained aloud. 'I'd mortally hate to meet harder.'

He sighed, thrust Marshal Matt Gant from his mind, and concentrated on the already wearying business of putting one boot down after the other.

EIGHT

DYING TIME

The buckskin was worse than winded; it had been run clear off its feet.

Gant hated to use a horse up that way, yet he'd had no choice. But the sheriff's long-legged saddler had done the job asked of it, and done it well. It had carried him up the steep, ravine-scarred face of the Catamount Hills, and now the job was done, the lawman forced himself to strip off saddle and bridle and give the horse a quick but comprehensive rubdown with the curry comb from the sheriff's saddle-bag.

By the time he was through the buckskin was breathing easier. Gant patted the sleek neck, then turned the animal's head back in the direction of the little spring they'd passed several hundred yards back and slapped it across the rump. The animal started off at a stubborn plod, but picked up its gait sharply once it caught the scent of the water.

Gant strode across to the Countess, fitted boot to stirrup and swung up. The mare was a little foot-sore from the long night ride and the climb, but still had plenty of stamina left, like her rider.

The sun hammered down hard as horse and rider quit the sparse shelter of the ridge trees and headed out for a broad rocky shelf. The marshal had already removed his jacket, and his shirtsleeves fluttered in the hot winds blowing steadily from the west.

The lowland south of the Catamounts began to unfold before him as the trees fell away behind. In the summer haze, the whole landscape seemed to smoke, stretching away in yellows and browns toward the Funeral Mountains under a brassy sky. From someplace far below, he picked up the faint metallic clanking of a windmill.

Soon the Lazy K Ranch lay almost directly below. The headquarters comprised ranch-house, barn, corral and stables. Two saddled horses stood at the hitchrail before the house. Identification at that distance was impossible, yet he was next door to certain that one of the tied animals was a roan.

A jerk on the lines brought his horse's head about and Gant set her upon the downtrail.

The south side of the Catamounts here was easier than the north, but the trail was still far too rough and uncertain to be travelled at speed. Nonetheless, Gant kept the black mare to a swift walking pace. He rode intent upon the trail, ready to kick free the moment his mount gave the first hint she might stumble and fall. Yet the Countess seemed to sense his urgency and fought to keep both her feet and her balance, neatly side-stepping the danger spots and dancing lightly over the shifting gravel.

He shot a quick glance behind.

He realized he was raising plenty dust. But he was banking upon the Tuckers being too involved and preoccupied with their business at the house to be keeping a tight watch on the hills.

With the worst of the ride behind him now, Gant found the decline beginning to slope away more gradually. He was passing through scrubby jackpine that cut off sight of the spread. Eventually Countess crested a dusty knoll, and the Lazy K headquarters lay in clear view less than a mile ahead.

The horses were still there, and he could see Jimmy Tucker running towards them toting a gunnysack.

Dust rose from the mare's hoofs as he jerk-reined her to a halt. Tucker was lashing the gunnysack to the pommel of his roan. Now Gant sighted Rebecca emerging from behind the barn leading two horses on catch ropes. The girl was hurrying, bending sharply forward from the waist as she led the animals towards the front of the house.

The face of the lawman showed nothing as he sat in his saddle, watching. Yet behind that unchanging mask, Matt Gant was tasting regret. It was almost as if, somewhere deep inside his subconscious, he'd been secretly hoping not to find them here.

Such thinking was so foreign to his ruthless nature that it jolted him and took him a spell to recover. Stoneface Gant feeling sympathy for a convicted killer? That didn't even begin to seem right.

'You're just played out, Gant,' he told himself grimly. 'Hell! You're overtired and are too stubborn to admit it. But you'd better grab some genuine rest before you get back to Chisum or you'll start coming apart. . . .'

The Tuckers left the horses at the tierack and hurried inside. Gant sensed they were on the verge of pulling out.

A light pressure of the knees sent Countess through the last of the trees. Once in the open, he moved her into a lope, his Buntline Special in his hand glittering in the sunlight now; his stubbled jaw was set rock hard as he rode.

His eyes bored at the house, watching for the first sign that would warn him he'd been spotted.

He was all purpose now. Yet again came an un-Gant-like thought; he hoped that fool boy wouldn't try to make a fight of it.

A hundred yards separated the rider from the house before a startled face appeared at a rear window. The face vanished and Gant booted the black mare into an instant gallop. Sweeping through the ranchyard gate, gun upraised and eyes glittering, he filled his lungs and bellowed a shout that was deliberately meant to terrify.

'Tucker! Come out with your hands up! You don't stand a chance!'

Rushing down the south side of the house, making for the hitchrail, he heard the stutter of running feet from within. The Buntline thundered to drive a warning bullet through the roof. Shattered wooden slates tumbled over the front guttering as he wheeled around the corner and immediately slewed to a dust-boiling halt between the low porch and the tethered horses. Looking huge and frightening with heavy shoulders straining against the seams of his shirt, the lawman trained his weapon on the open doorway.

'Tucker! Don't make me come in after you, boy!'

He heard the girl cry out, then caught a blur of movement beyond a curtained window. Every instinct urged him to jump down and cease presenting a sitting target of himself. He should dismount and charge in there – the logical procedure in such a situation. But he couldn't and didn't; the girl was in there.

So, ignoring the risk he was taking, he kept to his saddle and shouted again; 'Last chance, Tucker! Think of your sister if you won't think of yourself!'

A hanging moment, then came Rebecca Tucker's voice: 'We're coming out, Marshal. Don't shoot!'

'Then come out and be quick about it!'

Steps sounded and the girl suddenly appeared in the doorway. She was pale and shaking and the look she gave Gant went through him like a knife.

Rebecca refused to move again until he gestured impatiently with the six-gun. He looked for Tucker behind her, but the doorway stood empty. A warning chill coursed down the back of his neck, but as his glance cut to the window, the girl came swiftly forward.

'Stand back!' he warned. 'Get—'

'Now, Jimmy!' she screamed, and lunged at the horse's head. The animal reared back and Gant was unbalanced for a vital moment. From the corner of his eye, he caught movement away to his right. The Buntline whipped round in that direction and Gant's eyes snapped wide.

Jimmy Tucker stood crouched at the corner, glaring at him over the barrel of a six-gun.

With the mare nervously unsteady beneath him, Gant knew he couldn't aim and fire before that menacing weapon exploded. Even so, he tried. But then, with the weapon firmly locked on its target, finger tight on the steel curve of the trigger, he realized Jimmy Tucker wasn't going to shoot. It was in the boy's eyes, and when the boy met Gant's hard stare, the weapon in his fist began to angle downwards.

'Shoot, Jimmy!' screamed the girl. 'Shoot him!'

The boy's face was sheened by cold sweat by this and the tension ran out of his slender shoulders.

'I can't, Sis,' he panted. 'I just can't. . . .'

She rushed to his side while Gant glared at the boy, not with relief but, paradoxically, with anger

104

blazing in his eyes.

'Why didn't you shoot, Tucker? Why?'

Her hands on her brother's shoulders, a distraught Rebecca swung her tear-stained face towards the lawman.

'He couldn't do it because he's not a killer and never was. You're fortunate it wasn't me with the weapon, Marshal Gant, for I would surely have pulled the trigger. Better a man like you to perish than my brother who never hurt anybody in his life ... a thousand times better—'

Her voice broke and Tucker reached out and took her in his arms, still clutching the weapon as he stared over her head at the lawman.

It was a long moment before Gant could muster the energy to swing down. He moved like an old man as he crossed to the couple to take the six-shooter from Jimmy Tucker's unprotesting grip. He eased the hammer down off the cock with his thumb and stood staring at it dumbly, listening to the girl sobbing. This was a moment, yet all he felt was bad.

A gust of wind brought a dust devil dancing across the hard-packed sand of the yard. The sun hammered Gant's back. He stood with head bowed, so many conflicting emotions churning through him he was unable to make sense of any of them. All he knew for certain was that at that moment he would rather have been just about anyplace else, doing anything, than standing there listening to Rebecca Tucker weep.

*

Gant had decided they should wait out the worst of the day's brutal heat at the house, and it was mid afternoon before the party set off on the long return journey to Chisum.

Ten miles were covered in almost total silence, the Tuckers riding side by side, Gant behind them. The Catamounts fell slowly away to the right, then they crossed the tiny trickle of King John Creek and the hot, gusty wind of the plains was in their faces.

The party was passing through a line of deep, dry arroyos some thirty minutes later when Gant detected a subtle change in the atmosphere. Gazing at the sun, he saw that it had grown red and angry-looking. Countess lifted her handsome head and whickered. He patted her neck, then hipped around in the saddle to gaze at the mountains. A soft curse dropped from his lips. There was a growing smudge of cloud on the horizon to the south, and a ridge of thunderheads was churning and billowing against the shoulders of the Funerals. Even as he stared, the rumble of thunder muttered in the distance.

'Rain coming,' he called to the riders ahead. 'We'll push a little faster and maybe get to outrun it!'

The Tuckers heeled their mounts into a lope and Gant followed suit. Countess was willing enough but the lawman could tell by her gait that she was weary.

'We're not gonna outride this one, Marshal!' Jimmy Tucker yelled back several minutes later. 'And it looks like a mean one. Better find someplace to wait it out.'

'Keep riding!' Gant rapped.

Another half-mile and a vast shadow raced across the plains, enveloping the three riders, then rushing on ahead of them as tumbling cloud masses covered half the sky, swallowing the sun. The thunder grew louder and lightning worked in the clouds. A sudden gust of hot wind rushed over them and seized a distant grove of cottonwoods, rippling shapes across the trees like massive fingers at play.

Gant tugged a poncho from a saddlebag and was about to pull it on when he realized the Tuckers weren't packing any weather gear. Instantly, he kicked Countess across to draw level with the girl. He silently proffered the slicker. He half-expected her to reject his offer but instead she actually half-smiled as she took it from him. Back at the house, he'd been impressed by the way Rebecca had quickly regained her composure, and at the moment there seemed to be little resentment or anger in either of them now. It was as if both had accepted the inevitable, perhaps even come to understand he was merely doing his job. Maybe.

Minutes later the storm struck with full fury.

At first merely a few fat drops fell upon the dusty trail, then suddenly the world around them was obliterated by teeming walls of rain with thunder that deafened the ears.

Gant stuck it out for several violent minutes, then suddenly pushed his mount up between the couple.

'You know of any cover hereabouts, Tucker?' he shouted above the furious roaring voice of the storm.

'There's a canyon off to the right about a mile or so ahead,' Jimmy shouted back. 'Couple of decent sized caves there!'

'Good enough. Let's make time!'

Within a violent ten minutes, as the storm lashed down with ever-increasing fury, the three were within the shelter of a roomy dry cavern that was more than spacious enough to accommodate their mounts as well. Tucker found some dry sticks and twigs in the lee of a rocky overhang and they soon had a small fire going. They stood around the flames, steam rising from sodden clothing. The warmth here was pleasant, for the storm had sent the temperature plummeting.

After they'd dried off some, Gant broke out coffee and pot and quickly brewed up. Soon they were seated upon boulders drinking hot coffee and listening to the savage crackle of the lightning, punctuated by shuddering thunderclaps.

As time passed, Rebecca and her brother started quietly discussing inconsequential things, such as how badly the country needed rain, and whether or not there would be enough to flood the rivers. Matt Gant sat motionless, smoking a cheroot, listening, and watching, unwilling to make room for some of those disturbing thoughts that had been nagging at the edges of his mind following the recapture at the Lazy K.

Eventually Jimmy rose and strolled to the lip of the cavern to watch the rain. Rebecca set her pannikin aside, then drew a silver-backed comb from her pocket. She worked the comb slowly through her hair then drew the tresses to the nape of her neck where she fastened them with a mother-of-pearl clip.

This style, he noted, with the hair drawn back tightly to the sides of the head, emphasized the size and shape of the blue eyes which he seemed to find disconcerting whenever they might focus on him. At length, satisfied with her handiwork, the girl put the comb away, turned and faced him directly.

'You appear troubled, Marshal Gant.'

'I do?'

She nodded. 'I wonder if I can guess why?'

'Guessing doesn't cost anything.'

'You're beginning to have doubts, aren't you?'

'About what?'

'Jimmy, of course.'

'Juries have doubts, Miss Tucker. And judges. A federal marshal never does. Or at least he shouldn't.'

'Nonetheless, I'm still certain I'm right about you and your doubts, perhaps even grave ones. You are no longer sure whether you are involved in this case because Jimmy was found guilty of murder, or whether you're doing what you are doing because my father once injured and humiliated you.'

She linked hands around her knees and met Gant's stony stare without flinching. 'You haven't yet told me I'm wrong, Marshal Gant.'

109

'You're wasting your time, Miss Tucker. Maybe I'm prepared to admit your brother does seem to be different from what I expected. Maybe a lot different. But that doesn't change anything. The law has made its decision in his case, and I'm merely the instrument of that law.'

'And, of course, you believe the law can never be in error, don't you. That it must never be broken, shouldn't even be bent a little?'

'Of course.'

'Well, in that case, you should know you'll be jailing me when we get to Chisum, won't you?'

'I haven't said I would.'

'But you must. I was helping Jimmy. I begged him to shoot you back at the ranch. I mightn't know much about the law, Marshal, but I know that what I did warrants punishment. So, therefore, you must intend to lock me up.'

Gant held her steady gaze for a long moment, then dropped his gaze. 'No,' he said unevenly, 'I'm not bringing any charges against you.'

'But, Marshal, that's bending the rules. You can't simply—'

'Just what are you trying to do, Miss Tucker?' he snapped angrily.

She met his glare levelly.

'Perhaps I'm trying to show you that under that shell you've built around yourself is a man and not a machine. I've sensed that from the outset, and I'm more certain of it than ever at this moment. You like

110

me and feel sorry for me – I see it in your face. Yet you feel you can't give into your feelings for fear people might think you're human after all. And you are human, Marshal Gant, or at least you could be if you allowed yourself to be.'

He stared at her fixedly. He knew he could silence her with a harsh word if he chose. Yet he knew he would not, for deep down he wanted to believe every word she'd just said – wanted desperately to believe he wasn't a man of stone.

The taut moment held and lengthened. Then Jimmy said, 'Rain's easin' off.'

Gant turned to look out. The storm had indeed passed. There was now but a fine drizzle, while low in the west, the sun was struggling to peep through.

'Time to move,' he grunted, and without a backward glance, walked back to the horses.

Fifteen minutes found them well back on the trail again. Far ahead was to be seen the storm roiling and twisting away somewhere near Chisum. The sun shone brightly for an hour, then winked away into a long purple twilight before the first stars began to glimmer in a tranquil sky.

The miles drifted behind and were mighty long for Matt Gant as he travelled them, no longer totally preoccupied with what the days and nights might bring before the hanging. Neither did he brood on hostile towners, those rumors concerning Tom Bible, or the implied threat of Harley Raingo.

All he thought of was the girl who seemed to have

detected something in him that nobody else had done, a girl he wouldn't confine to prison even though he knew he should. For all he really wanted to do was to take her in his arms and protect her from even the gentlest wind that might brush against her cheek.

Rebecca Tucker had touched a secret place in the heart of the man some claimed had no heart at all.

Mud puddles reflected the glow of windows and street lamps as the bunch of weary riders rounded the corner of Hagan's Feed and Grain Store and headed towards the central block.

Two men stepped from the side door of a house, watched the party ride by, then began to follow them along the walk. Up ahead, one of the loafers on the porch of the Lady Jane darted off excitedly through the batwings, and moments later reappeared trailed by a number of men.

Gant twisted in the saddle to see that the two men following him in had been joined by several more. Amongst this bunch he spotted both Tom Jethro and Joe Ritchie.

The marshal's gaze cut sharply ahead to the law office. It stood in complete darkness. He realized the group on the porch of the Lady Jane had now swollen to roughly twenty. There was no noisy talk, yet he was conscious of a brooding, menacing quality in the rain-damp air of Trail Street.

His hand dropped to the butt of the Buntline

Special as they approached the Lady Jane. If there was interference of any kind he was ready for it. Solid ready.

The mob remained silent as the riders drew abreast, and Gant was beginning to relax some when somebody on the saloon porch moved forwards suddenly. He twisted in the saddle for a better look – and stared into the face of Tom Bible.

'Hold,' Gant said softly, and three horses drew to a halt.

'Marshal!' Rebecca Tucker whispered. 'That's Tom Bible. And those are some of his men in that group.'

'I know.' Gant didn't take his gaze from Bible, who stood with boots wideplanted and hands on hips, trading stare for stare. 'Tucker,' he said evenly, 'you and your sister ride across to the jailhouse and wait for me there.'

'Whatever you say, Marshal.'

'And . . . Tucker?'

'Yeah?'

'Don't attempt to take advantage of this situation. That would be dumb and dangerous.'

Jimmy Tucker made no reply. He nodded to Rebecca and both started in the direction of the law office, leaving Gant alone in the center of the muddy street.

The silence intensified.

The lawman's gaze flickered over the faces visible beyond Bible. He identified two known Bible riders,

113

hatchet-faced Dave Kells and blocky Olan Jackson.

At last Tom Bible spoke.

'Seems to me all of a sudden you ain't got much to say for yourself for a feller they reckon talks up a blue streak, Gant.'

The outlaw unfolded heavy arms. He was a big man with broad shoulders, his face pale and pock-marked, with eyes set viciously close together over a broken nose. His attire was nondescript but for the gunrig. The heavy belt, the holsters and the twin guns were all well cared for. The man radiated danger the way a skunk stinks.

'Yeah, where's all the biggety talk now, Gant?' hooted Tom Jethro. 'Seems to me that—'

'Shut your mouth!'

Gant's warning bounced back from the false-fronts. He swung Countess to face the Lady Jane with his fingers still caressing gunbutt. His hard eyes drilled at Bible.

'You're bucking for trouble, Bible, so I'm giving you a choice. Unbuckle your guns or use them.'

The outlaw's eyes widened momentarily at such a challenge, then narrowed dangerously.

'You don't seem to understand, lawdog. You ain't just buckin' me and the boys – you got yourself a whole dang town up against you now.'

Gant made no reply. The street was hushed. Relishing his big moment, the gunman moved forward to raise one boot to a brick step.

'You see, hot shot, I just couldn't believe it when I

114

heard that old stone-face Gant had brung that kid
back here and was fixin' to hang him in Chisum. I
called the feller that brung me that news a baldy-
faced liar, on account I wouldn't believe even a stiff-
necked grand-stander like yourself would ever be
that loco.'

He waited for response but Gant remained silent,
didn't move in his saddle.

Bible flushed and inflated his barrel of a chest.
'Okay, seems I was wrong. Looks like you are that
loco, badge-toter, but this here is my town and it's
always been the place where me and my boys can
relax some and sip a little rye whiskey in peace and
quiet without no big-nosed badge-toter hornin' in
and that's how she stays. Only trouble, me and my
pards just never could relax right in no town with the
stink of a mongrel-gutted tinstar in the air . . . so that
means you gotta go – one way or the other!'

The outlaw paused to gaze around and see how
the mob was enjoying it all, and they appeared to be
liking it just fine. That was how Gant assessed things
also, for these were surely low-life scum to whom
somebody like Bible was like a shining beacon. But
where lawman and badman differed was in their
assessment of the caliber of the man in the street in
this town. Bible believed he had backing, Gant
doubted it. In truth Gant thought this so strongly, he
had no hesitation in saying so.

'If you are counting on these to back your play,
Bible,' he replied in a voice that carried, 'you're a

bigger fool than I thought. Half of these men are pack runners – gutless scum. They tried to mob me the night I came here and every one turned to water. So, maybe the odds are still your way. But think on this. If we come to it, you're the first one I'll get for sure – you can make book on that. If they get me later you're not going to know about it – small time!'

'I guess we've jawed enough, lawdog!' came the hissed reply. 'All right, boys let's cut this grand-stander down to size and—'

It was at that moment a sharp shout came from the upper gallery of the Chuckwagon Hotel.

'The first man that draws his gun gets a bellyfull of buckshot!'

All heads turned. In plain view, Sheriff Bragg and Judge Nimrod stood upon the hotel balcony. Bragg clutched a double-barreled shotgun in unsteady hands while the judge was scowling down on the mob over an old-fashioned pepperbox pistol. The two had four armed towners standing in back of them, grim jawed and ready for anything.

'You heard the sheriff!' Nimrod shouted into the stunned silence. 'The first man to draw against the marshal gets a bellyfull of buckshot.'

Gant was as incredulous as anybody present, with maybe the exception of Bible. For a long moment it appeared that the unexpected turn of events would see the bad man cave in. And maybe it would have done had not Bible taken the precaution of downing three double shots beforehand to lend himself that

116

extra ounce of courage he'd feared he might need when he stook his stand tonight.

The double ryes boosted his courage as desired – but crippled his judgment. Flushed and enraged, the wild man cursed and went for his guns, mad eyes blazing down at the marshal.

Gant drew and triggered in one silken motion. Tom Bible staggered and crashed down dead with a sudden third eye in the center of his forehead. Kells and Jackson were coming clear as Bragg's shotgun exploded with a roar. His jittery aim was poor and the double charge of buckshot riddled the porch a good six feet from Jackson, Kells and the sprawled Bible. Yet the shotgun's deafening blast played havoc with the nerves of hardcases already demoralized by Tom Bible's fall, and before they could get their guns working the town-tamer's Buntline was again singing its death song.

Jackson fell first, nose-diving into the muddy street. Dave Kells touched off one wild bullet before lead stitched across his chest, hammering him backwards. The window of the saloon exploded before the weight of his falling body and Kells went through in a shower of glass, dead legs hooked over the sill.

'You all right, Marshal?' Mel Bragg called down.

Gant nodded, then turned. Jimmy and Rebecca sat in their saddles before the jailhouse, ashen with shock, frozen.

A ragged breath broke from Gant's chest. They'd

not tried to run . . . while a deadbeat sheriff and a joke of an old judge had risked their lives to stand up for him. He found it all hard to believe, only knew it felt good as he slid the Buntline back into leather. Suddenly exhausted, he could feel his shoulders slumping as he turned his horse for the jailhouse. Rebecca made to speak to him as he moved past to dismount stiffly, but something in his face held her silent.

Porchboards creaked beneath his weight as he moved to the jailhouse door. 'Come on, son,' he said in a voice barely recognizable as his own. 'Reckon we've still got one sound cell left.'

Rebecca reached out and touched her brother's hand. Then she watched Jimmy dismount and climb onto the porch landing. The young man paused, stared blankly at the marshal, then stepped past him. Gant stared at the girl in silence, then followed Jimmy inside. To the silent onlookers, the town-tamer of Chisum looked every inch the enforcer and hero, while Matt Gant himself felt like a man who had stayed on for one town and one gunfight too many.

NINE

GALLOWS IN
THE SUN

It looked a fine day for a hanging.

The gray morning light brightened at the approach of the sun to a vast arch of a sky without a single cloud. Gradually the distant peaks of the Funeral Mountains began to glow, catching the first beams of the still-hidden sun. The mountain peaks seemed to float in the sky, unconnected to the earth below.

Then the blood-red sun came surging over the horizon and the world was flooded with light. The floating pyramids of fire became the iron walls of the Funerals, and another blistering day was on the march.

The day they would hang Jimmy Tucker.

Crimson daubed the waiting gallows that stood gaunt and tall in the center of the unfamiliarly tidy quarter-acre behind Parnell's Mercantile. The edifice which the accused's friends had thrown up on the marshal's orders was less sturdy than the one they'd burned down, but it was solid enough and would do the job required of it.

The day's first rays fell upon the mountainous bulk of the man in the shiny black suit making his way along Trail Street from the hotel. Milton Gotham's shoes squeaked painfully, sounding like little live things were being crushed under the burden of his three hundred pounds. A fat black valise swung from a pudgy hand. The hangman had purchased a new length of rope for the Chisum assignment and was on his way to fit it to the gibbet. The hanging wasn't scheduled until nine, but Gotham was a meticulous man who didn't believe in leaving things until the last minute.

In her room at the Chuckwagon Hotel, Rebecca Tucker stood by her window watching the sun break free of the horizon. She was fully dressed. She had not closed her eyes during the longest night of her life. In her eyes, the sun appeared to be rushing into the sky, hurrying towards nine o'clock as if it could not wait to witness the hanging.

At the Diamond Spot Café, Sheriff Mel Bragg and Judge Nimrod sat at a window table spooning sugar into hot coffee. Charlie the Greek, owner of the Diamond Spot, had not closed his doors all night.

It seemed that nobody had slept in Chisum. At all hours through the night men were to be seen moving slowly along the walks, or standing talking softly in groups. There had been no anger, no sense of excitement. The bloody shoot-out at the Lady Jane two nights earlier had seemed to drain wild Chisum of all emotion other than a kind of chilling dread.

There were a few who still hoped that by some miracle the hanging would not take place, yet most were resigned to the fact that Gant would do exactly what he'd come here to do, namely, execute a convicted killer and hammer home the iron fact that law and order was back to stay.

In his cell, Jimmy Tucker watched as the sun threw the barred shape of his single window against the far wall. The condemned had shaved, yet the little nicks along his jaw testified that his hands had been shaky. A pale blue shirt, moleskin pants and brown range boots comprised the outfit he would wear on his last walk on earth. He smoked a cigarette and tasted nothing.

The shades of the front office were still drawn, admitting only thin slivers of sunlight through the cracks. The room, filled with cigar smoke, was gloomy and still. Gant was seated behind the spur-scarred desk, the cigar in the ash tray before him sending up a thin plume of pale-blue smoke into the stale air.

The lawman's face was haggard, with dark shadows under the eyes and deep creases in the cheeks. The marshal had not slept that night. He still had the look of a man hewn out of rock, yet there was a hint of something undercutting the stone someplace.

Time passed.

121

Then all of a sudden, Chisum jolted fully awake and men began to converge on Gallows Corner to watch Milton Gotham testing the trap with a sandbag. A crowd gathered across the street from the jailhouse. Eight o'clock came and went. Eight-thirty. The watchers in the street were focused upon the jailhouse now, waiting for marshal and prisoner to appear. A stir rippled through the watchers as Rebecca Tucker came from the hotel in a plain dark dress and crossed to the law office. She was admitted by the marshal and the door closed again.

'It's gone twenty to nine,' Shad Fellows muttered, consulting his fine pocket watch. 'Why doesn't he get it over and done with? This waiting until the last minute can only be making it harder on Jimmy.'

The eyes that flicked at the rancher were cold and unfriendly. Fellows had never been a popular man in Chisum, and his stocks had plummeted ever since he'd gone off to Sacramento City to testify against Jimmy Tucker. Inured to their hostility by this, Fellows closed his watch and adopted a look that told the world he'd merely done what he reckoned to be right. An honest man's duty could be painful at times, that long-faced look said, but that was no reason to shirk it.

Abruptly the jailhouse door swung open and the girl emerged. Necks craned for a glimpse of Jimmy, but there was still no sign of either the boy or the marshal.

Eventually they heard wheels upon gravel from the

far end of the block and turned to see a fast-moving buckboard swinging around the corner of the Feed and Grain Barn.

It was obvious by the erratic gait of the horse in the shafts that it was run off its legs, yet the driver continued to lash at the lathered rump with the lines as he came on down the central block.

'Who's that fool usin' up a hoss thataway?' Grover Parnell growled.

'That's Tim Bodie of the Lazy K,' Brawn Carter said. 'But who's that feller with him?'

The man seated at the ranch-hand's side was plainly old with a flowing white beard and silver hair. There was an impressive dignity in his bearing and a biblical cast to the large, well-shaped head as he sat staring directly ahead, paying no attention to the watchers on either side.

'Hey! I know that old feller,' Miles Lester suddenly exclaimed. 'That's Moses Brown from the Funerals.' The man paused, then his eyes widened as a thought hit. 'Hey! Jimmy Tucker claims he was visitin' old Moses when he was supposed to have shot—'

Lester broke off as the man standing beside him began backing away hastily. 'Hey, where do you think you're off to, Fellows?'

Fellows made no response. The man was now quite pale as he turned and began walking away, but Lester hastened after him, his expression suddenly suspicious.

Then Tim Bodie shouted from the buckboard as it

drew abreast, 'Hey! Grab hold of that bastard, somebody! He's the one who tried to lie Jimmy into a noose!'

Men started after the rancher in a rush. Wild-eyed now, Fellows broke into a run just as Gant appeared across the way in the jailhouse doorway.

'What the devil is going on over there?' the lawman shouted.

Gant's shout appeared to terrify Shad Fellows. The man stumbled on a loose plank in the boardwalk, shot a wild glance over one shoulder, then grabbed at the gun on his hip.

Gant's reaction was blistering fast. His gun leapt into his fist and he punched a bullet into the wall of the store inches over Fellows's head. 'The next one won't miss!' Gant warned. 'Get your hand off that gun!'

Fellows stood in a crouch, frozen by indecision, his gun half clear of leather. Before he could make a decision, burly Brawn Carter reached him from behind. A big hand closed over Fellows's wrist and shook it loose from the gun. Fellows cursed and swung a wild punch at the big man's head, but the blow was arrested as Miles Lester came up from behind and snared the flailing arm, capturing him.

'Bring that man over here!' Gant shouted angrily. Then he turned back to the buckboard and finally got a clear sighting of the old man in flowing robes stepping down.

'Moses!'

'Ahh, Gant, my son,' the oldster said with

impressive dignity. 'Tell me, have we arrived in time?'

'Jimmy is still alive, Moses,' Rebecca cried, hurrying to the old man, both hands extended. 'Oh, thank God Tim found you, Moses – thank God!'

Moses seized the girl's hands and smiled. Despite his impressive silver-haired age, there was a robustness about the way the man moved with more than a hint of power still in his big arms. Moses Brown dwelt in caverns up in the mountains, subsisting on herbs and berries which he proclaimed to be life-extending. He could quote the Bible word-perfect and was considered by those privileged to know him as a holy man of great wisdom.

One of those people wore a marshal's badge upon his dark coat, and there was something like hope in the lawman's eyes as he approached the older man.

'Moses,' he greeted. 'What brings you here?'

The old man released Rebecca's hand. He turned away for a moment to watch the towners who were struggling to bring Fellows across to the jailhouse, then faced the marshal. He reached out and clapped a gnarled hand upon the lawman's shoulder.

'What brings me? Why, the hope of saving the life of an innocent boy, Matt.' He spread his hands. 'And it could only be a miracle that sees me here, my son, for I have been wandering for weeks alone through the mountains, seeking the truth in the hearts of flowers and washing my ancient body in the Maker's pure streams. It was only by chance I happened upon Tim when he was camped in a glade last night . . .

125

and there he told me the whole terrible story.'

'About Jimmy, you mean?'

'Of course. If we hadn't met, then that fine young boy would have had his life taken away from him – executed for a crime of which he knows nothing.'

'But how can you be sure of that, Moses?'

Moses stared him straight in the eye. 'Jimmy Tucker was with me throughout the twenty-fourth and twenty-fifth of July, Matt.' He placed one hand over his heart. 'I swear this by the Lord I love more than life itself.'

'He's lyin'!' Shad Fellows shouted. 'Gant, you can't take the word of a crazy old cracker like this!'

But Shad Fellows was wrong about that. Gant was willing to stake his life that everything the old mountain mystic said was true; he was a man incapable of falsehood.

And yet he instantly knew this wasn't going to be easy. Violent Chisum was primed up for a hanging, and glancing about him now he could see how many were angered by this latest development. But this made no difference to the marshal of Chisum; he could not permit it to do so.

The marshal's face had turned cold as he turned on his heel to stare at Shad Fellows. 'You lied, Fellows!' he accused. 'You lied under oath and almost cost an innocent man his life! Why?'

'You're a fool, Gant!' Fellows shot back, leathery cheeks flushing hectically. 'What the hell reason would I have to lie—?'

'Maybe for the reason that Jimmy put to me,' Gant interrupted. 'You saw your chance of taking over the Lazy K, and maybe even getting to wed Rebecca with her brother out of the way?'

'That was why you lied, wasn't it, Shad?' Rebecca chimed in. 'It could be the only possible reason!'

'Rebecca, don't do this to me,' Fellows groaned. 'You know I love you – know I would never do anything in the world to hurt you!'

'I know you would do anything to get what you want,' was the girl's cold response.

Then her eye fell upon the face of the Chain Ranch ramrod amongst the rapidly swelling crowd. 'Omega, surely you must know that Shad lied at the trial.'

Omega Huck ducked his head low and began pushing back through the mob before Gant's powerful voice halted him in his tracks.

'Come back here, mister. Pronto!'

A tall and rawboned man with thick sandy hair and bushy eybrows, Omega Huck flicked one fearful glance at Fellows, then began shouldering his way through the mob again.

'You just keep your big mouth shut, Huck!' Fellows warned.

'No, you shut yours, mister,' Gant stated grimly. He drilled the ramrod with a hard eye as he mounted the porch. 'I want the truth from you, mister, and you'll let me have it or else—'

'I don't know nothin', Marshal,' Huck insisted,

tucking both hands tightly under his armpits in an attempt to hide their sudden trembling. 'Honest.'

'Have you ever been in prison, Huck?'

The man's eyes popped. 'Judas! No I ain't, Marshal. Hell, I ain't never been run in even for bein' drunk!'

'You'd be surprised how quick that can change if you try playing games with me. It's plain to me Fellows lied to the judge and jury at Tucker's trial. If this is proved, Fellows will feel the full weight of the law, as will be the fate of anyone with knowledge of his crime. Understand? If you know anything about this matter, speak up now or suffer the consequences, which could even see you fetch as much as ten years behind bars.'

Gant was exaggerating but Omega Huck had no way of knowing that.

'I swear I had nothin' to do with it, Marshal Gant,' he blurted. 'Heck, I wasn't even there when Mr Fellows and Hec Oliver got to—'

The man broke off abruptly, realizing he'd gone too far. He attempted to look back at Fellows who was snarling at him to shut up, but Gant seized him by the shirt front and dragged his face close to his own.

'When Shad Fellows and Hec Oliver did what, cowhand?'

Heck blinked into Gant's eyes as if hypnotized. 'Why . . . when . . . when they tangled, Marshal.'

'What about?'

'Oliver done the boss outa some money—'

'And they had a fight?'

128

'Yeah.'

'And?'

The ramrod swallowed. Painfully. 'And . . . and the boss man shot him!'

Gant released his grip. He stood staring at Huck for a long moment while the hushed crowd gaped in disbelief. Then, without even a glance in Fellows's direction, he swung and vanished through the jailhouse doorway. A buzz rippled through the crowd as they waited. It wasn't long before a great cheer went up as an unshackled Jimmy Tucker appeared in the doorway, blinking as though dazed.

The minutes that followed were chaotic, with Jimmy and his weeping sister embracing, men crowding forward to clap the boy on the back, while Mel Bragg and Brawn Carter struggled to muscle an ashen-faced Shad Fellows through the noisy mob and into the jailhouse.

Through all this, Matt Gant stood off to one side, his expression remote and distant as if none of this any longer concerned him. Moses Brown came across to speak to him, but drawing no response the old man shrugged and turned away. Then Bragg approached to ask if the marshal wanted Fellows charged with murder and was told, almost indifferently, that it was up to him.

After Bragg disappeared back inside, scratching his head and burdened down by the weight of new responsibility, Jimmy and Rebecca, arms about one another, crossed to where Gant was standing.

'No hard feelin's, Marshal?' Jimmy grinned.

A faint frown creased the lawman's brow. 'What was that?'

Jimmy thrust out his right hand. 'Just wanted you to know I don't bear any grudge, Marshal. I figure you only did what you thought was right. And I'll never forget you could have gunned me twice, but you didn't. And, hell, I guess now it's over, I don't even believe you were out to square accounts for what the old man did to you after all. So, can we call it quits?'

Gant frowned down at the outstretched hand, but made no move to claim it before Rebecca spoke.

'Please, Marshal, it would mean so much to both of us.'

The lawman met her eyes levelly. The scowl began to fade. Then his right extended and claimed the boy's in a powerful grip. Disbelief and excitement gripped the crowd at this, and the Tuckers were all relieved smiles before they were claimed by others eager to offer their congratulations now.

It wasn't long before somebody decided that a drink was called for. The jailhouse porch emptied magically. Gant stood off to one side watching as men hoisted Jimmy Tucker onto their shoulders and toted him off for the Lady Jane where saloon-keeper Big Hannigan was sufficiently moved by it all to break the tight-fisted habits of a lifetime in announcing a round of free drinks.

The marshal extracted a crooked black cigar from his vest and was setting it alight when an enormous figure appeared from Peach Street beneath a big white sun hat, looking for all the world like a petulant child who'd just had his candy bar taken away.

Milton Gotham glared across the street at the jailhouse then started across. Yet such was the flinty stare Gant drilled at the hangman that he faltered, then stopped to stare blinking and uncertain in the yellow glare of Trail Street, before eventually turning away.

Gant didn't turn at the familiar sound of boots in the doorway behind him.

'Marshal?'

No answer.

Bragg emerged to stand alongside. 'Marshal, will I arrange to bring Fellows up before the judge? I mean . . . well, I guess I know he's as guilty as hell. But I figger after what's happened we got to have us a hearin' here afore we can lodge the official charge in Sacramento City, huh?'

'Your affair, Sheriff, not mine.'

'But—' Bragg broke off as the lawman made to move away. 'Hey, where you goin', Marshal?'

'Nowhere in particular, Sheriff.'

But the marshal lied. He knew exactly where he was going and what he was going to do.

The afternoon's late shadows were stretching across the lot in back of Parnell's Mercantile when the ponderous figure under the huge white hat came trudging diconsolately through the dust and heat of

Gallows Corner.

Several of Hortense Crackley's small fry scuttled out from underneath the gallows and scampered away.

The hangman didn't even seem to notice. It had been a bitterly disappointing day and his spirits were at a low ebb. Not only had he been deprived of his hour in the limelight and a fifty-dollar fee that morning, but he'd just learned that a prima facie case had been established against Shad Fellows by Judge Nimrod, with arrangements already in train to transport Fellows to Sacramento City under escort to stand trial there.

Gotham had stayed on the offchance the citizenry would be sufficiently angered about Fellows maybe to stage their own trial and find their man guilty, in which case they would find themselves in need of his specialized talents. He surely hated to waste a fine sunny day and a brand new rope. But his hopes had proven groundless and now there was nothing for it but to go pack up and head for home.

The gallows' steps groaned beneath his great weight as he climbed up onto the platform. He'd left his rope looped around a crossbeam – just in case. He shook his head as he tested the trapdoor with a big black boot. What a waste! He knew it would have been a hanging to remember.

He sighed again and was reaching up for his rope when something landed upon his hat. His head jerked upwards to sight the evil-eyed red rooster perched arrogantly atop the crossbeam. Slowly, disgustedly, Gotham removed his proud white sombrero and examined the damage done. His ponderous lower lip began to tremble. What a hell of a day!

Some time later, toting his unused rope and desecrated hat, Milton Gotham came plodding down the sturdy steps, and made his way back across the lot. Behind and above, the rooster strutted along the crossbeam silhouetted against the crimson glow of sunset, crowing and cackling derisively. To the ear of the Territorial hangman, the screeching sounded like a mocking harpy from Hell.

Mel Bragg sat alone at the law office desk. Around eight o'clock, Judge Nimrod appeared, coming through the doorway with a bottle tucked beneath one arm and his crutch under the other, left pants leg neatly turned up and sewn like a sack across the bottom. Stiff and awkward with the crutch, Nimrod made his way to the vacant chair and sat down, grunting. He set the bottle between them and leaned his crutch against the desk.

'A long day, Sheriff.'

'Long day indeed, Judge.'

'Care for a shot?'

'Not right now, I reckon.'

'Funny thing, I don't feel that much like a drink myself.'

Bragg rubbed a hand over his face. The sheriff was

clean shaven. It even appeared as if he'd run a comb through his hair – carefully. People had been noticing that Mel Bragg appeared to be getting markedly more particular about himself ever since Matt Gant had come to town.

'You see the marshal, Judge?' Bragg asked after a silence.

'Yes. He's still at it.'

'Still drinkin', you mean?'

'Yes. Sitting by himself at the Last Hope with a bottle of brandy.'

'Drunk?'

'Didn't look it.'

The sheriff scowled. 'What do you figure's got into that man, Judge?'

'Who can guess? He's nothing like any breed of man you or I know anything much about, Sheriff.'

'I guess that's true enough. But . . . but you don't think he could be comin' apart, do you?'

'Ever see a lump of iron come apart?'

'Reckon not.'

'Well, you'll see that happen first before you see Gant fold up.' The judge leaned forward and picked up the bottle. The cork came out with a pop. He sniffed the contents, frowned, then recorked the whiskey and replaced it on the desk. 'Beats all,' he muttered. 'Of a sudden I seem to have lost my thirst, Bragg. But how could that be?'

Bragg offered no reply. But as they sat there in silence over an untouched bottle each man felt he understood the true reason why Chisum's notable boozers appeared to have lost their taste for the hard stuff recently.

On that day when Bible came to town to stir up things and lie in wait for the marshal, a half-drunk Nimrod and a well-primed Bragg had sat across this same desk and decided that if nobody else was prepared to do it, they should at least make a token effort to support Gant, his arrogance notwithstanding.

In retrospect, it might seem they hadn't been of all that great an assistance, yet they had assisted Gant a little and in doing so had improved their lagging status around town to a marked degree. Ever since that shoot-out, men had taken to tipping their hats to Bragg on the street, whereas before they were prone to pass him by without even appearing to see him.

It went even further than that.

These days, folks seemed more inclined to shut up and listen to Judge Nimrod when he lectured them on his pet topics of justice and fair play. And in earning the grudging admiration of the town, the sheriff and the judge realized they'd also earned something each man had imagined he'd long lost for good: self-respect.

So they sat in reflective silence in the little jailhouse, the man who'd shaved himself for a record five days running, and the booze-hound judge who appeared to have lost his notorious taste for strong drink.

While along at the Last Hope Saloon the man who'd helped to jolt them out of their dissolute way of life, and by example had shamed them into becoming better men than they'd known themselves to be, was ordering another bottle of Blue River Brandy.

It took a lot of brandy to assuage a fifteen-year thirst.

It had been that long since Matt Gant had last drunk his fill. There had never been more than one or two drinks at one time for a man who walked with danger every day of his life, whose strongest protection against his enemies was eternal vigilance.

Of course, there had been times aplenty in the past, after the guns had fallen silent and the losers laid in their graves, when the marshal had longed for the sweet solace of the bottle. Yet iron self-discipline and the eternal awareness that a killer with a gun could be lurking beyond the next corner always restricted him to take just the one, or perhaps two, but no more. Never any more.

That unknown man with the gun might well be waiting for him someplace here tonight, yet he still continued to put the hard stuff away, regardless.

Tonight he was no longer concerned about the danger without, but the danger within. For the first time in his career, he'd felt the iron substance that had molded Matthew Gant, Federal Marshal, show signs of crumbling and he realized he'd brought it upon himself.

He'd come to Chisum, faced a town down, walked

with danger every waking hour, braced Harley Raingo, run down a jail escaper and killed three men in a blazing shoot-out at the Lady Jane Saloon. During that time he'd gone sleepless for longer than he could remember . . . and also had come within a heartbeat of hanging an innocent man.

Yet the most damaging factor of all was the knowledge of how perilously close he'd come to making a mistake. All along, he'd denied to others and to himself that Jimmy Tucker's father had anything to do with his bringing Jimmy to this town to hang him.

He'd clung to that belief until the truth was revealed at the jailhouse. With Shad Fellows now exposed as the killer, he'd only then realized that Shep Tucker had had everything to do with it.

It was hate for the man who'd once shot him that had driven the man to seek revenge upon his son. He knew now that had the condemned been anybody but Shep Tucker's son he would have made a greater effort to investigate his claims of innocence.

Reviewing the whole affair in retrospect now he would concede that the boy had never really shaped up as any kind of killer right from the outset. Matt Gant usually had a sure feel for such things, an instinct. But in this case, hatred and exhaustion had caused him to disregard what his instincts were trying to tell him.

So he drank to repair the damage incurred in the longest week of his life. He drank to forget the men he'd killed here . . . and the way a girl's rain-damp hair shone by the glow of a camp-fire.

Then another jolt or two to ease the faint ache in his leg where he was once shot . . . then another for the weight in his heart. Erase them all, in order that he might become whole and invincible again before undertaking the ride to Sacramento City.

He would be returning only to turn in his badge but he was too proud to go back until fully restored as the man they knew, feared and respected. They would not be permitted to remember him as Matt Gant, played-out, self-doubting, on the drink. They would see him as he'd always been. The iron marshal.

He slept fifteen hours that night. He dreamed strange and gentle dreams of green acres and a man who worked cattle and horses and could plough a straighter furrow than any of his neighbours . . . a man who came home at night, not to a stark jailhouse or some dreary hotel room, but to a house made warm and welcoming by someone who could clearly see he was just a man behind that wall he'd thrown up around himself. . . .

He awoke to the realization that rest and good brandy had already done their healing work. He always healed fast. Another day and he would be ready to throw a saddle across Countess and hit the north trail.

The morning was already well under way by the time he'd shaved, dressed, taken coffee at the

Diamond Spot and fired up his first cigar of the day.

The day was sunny but lacked yesterday's fierce, driving heat. Men and women went about their everyday business and there seemed to be a quality in the air that was both new and strange to Chisum. There was visibly less hostility in the faces that passed him by, none of that brooding sense of menace he'd felt so powerfully upon first riding in.

It was almost as if the whole town had been purged of its poison by the events it had been exposed to over the past week. And who could tell? With the Bible gang no more and Mel Bragg at last beginning to shape up as a real sheriff, maybe Chisum had finally turned the corner. They had felt the full might of the law at last, seen their tarnished heroes fall, then witnessed the process of real justice in action. If all that combined to mold Chisum into a better place then perhaps it had all been worthwhile.

Yet he knew as he sat in the slanting sunlight which came pouring through the saloon windows, that when he left, part of himself would be left behind. He refused to identify the reason for this regret, for that would be out of character or might even be viewed as a sign of weakness.

Nonetheless, blue eyes seemed to appear before him in golden bars of sunlight as he lifted his glass and drank to the woman he knew he would never forget. . . .

TEN

GOING HOME

'Drinkin'?' Harley Raingo was disbelieving. 'I can't swallow that, Vestry. That stiff-necked Gant wouldn't drink enough in a whole year to pickle a frog!'

'Well, he was drinking yesterday, boy. Drinkin' and jest settin' around like a feller with nothin' to do and all year to do it in.'

Raingo studied his companion narrowly. 'You sayin' he was drunk?'

'Well, I ain't never said he was fallin' ass-over or anythin' like that. Reckon he's too full of hisself to be seen thataway. But he sure put aside enough to make any man drunk yesterday, though I seen him walkin' back to his hotel around midnight, steady as could be. Must have stone guts.'

Harley Raingo's hawk face was thoughtful as he pulled out his tobacco pouch. The two stood by their

140

mounts in late afternoon sunlight at a bend in the trail ten miles south of Chisum. Vestry, a cowhand by trade, was en route for the Double Star Ranch west of the Funeral Mountains to take a job punching steers when Raingo had ridden down from the high country. The gunman appeared shabby and sported a three-day growth, but still looked much the same as he had done during his brief and violent visit to Chisum.

'You ain't figurin' to start up with that there marshal again, are you, Raingo?' Vestry asked after a silence.

'Mebbe, mebbe not. But what of it if I was?'

'Well, that'd be none of my business, I reckon, pard. But if I was you I'd keep well clear of that hardnose. Okay, he might be lettin' his guard down some hittin' the booze thataway. But I'd still rather take my chances with the Spring Hill Apaches than mess with him.'

Black eyes flashed. 'Like you say, Vestry, it ain't none of your business what I'm doin'.'

Vestry ran a finger around his shirt collar. Raingo was acting proddy and mean. But following his experiences back in Chisum recently, Vestry reckoned he'd seen enough of this wild breed to last him a long spell.

'Well,' he said at last after another awkward silence, 'I'd best be gettin' on my way, Raingo. Want to get to the spread afore sundown.'

'Yeah, yeah,' the gunman said sourly, not looking

141

at him. 'Better hustle along, Vestry. Them cows mightn't wait.'

Raingo stared northwards in the direction of Chisum while Vestry was mounting. He didn't even turn when the other called goodbye and started off. along the trail.

Cigarette pasted to bottom lip, the hard man absently scratched at his ribs. He was neat by nature but hadn't had the chance to look after himself the way he liked over recent days. It was not his regular style to camp out in a cave and eat off what he could shoot, but that was what he'd been doing. Living rough while trying to decide whether to eat crow where the man who'd humiliated him that day in Arizona was concerned, or make another try at evening the score that had brought him a hundred miles to Chisum.

Standing there on the rutted road smoking his bitter cigarette, he knew he'd virtually decided in favor of taking the peaceful way out when he'd encountered Vestry riding by. He still wanted Gant dead the worst way; that hadn't changed. Yet just yesterday, he'd struck a drifter who'd actually witnessed Gant's gundown against the Bible bunch, and his description of that event had driven home to the gunpacker yet again that Matt Gant had to be about the last man in South-west Territory you'd want to mess with.

Yet what Vestry had just told him about Gant made him think again. The marshal on the booze? That

was surely something to whet a gunman's appetite.
Gant was good . . . nobody could argue that. But he
didn't believe any man living – Matt Gant or Wild Bill
Hickok – could load himself up with a skinful of
rotgut then stand against himself – double-fast
Harley Raingo.

All it would take was one sure bullet – one lousy
slug to erase that black day back in Arizona when
Gant had worked him over in a way that men still
whispered about behind his back. . . .

The cigarette scorched the gunfighter's lips. He
spat it out and slowly drew the back of his hand
across his mouth. Flexing supple shoulders he stared
at the dying sun and felt the tingle in his wrists that
was always reassuringly there whenever he was
considering some big and exciting job.

He smiled for the first time that day, all doubt
fading now. There was an old saying that no fast gun
living could ever count himself truly safe against one
determined man with a gun. Harley Raingo had seen
that adage proved out many a time in the past, and
he reckoned he could make it happen again tonight.

In Chisum.

'Another sarse, Marshal?'

Gant looked up from the empty glass to the face of
the bartender standing behind the bar in white
apron, bottle poised and smiling.

'No,' he replied soberly. 'Two sarsaparillas are my
limit these days,' he added, and the barman thought

he caught the hint of a half-smile. 'You may take my glass.'

The man moved away and Gant picked up his hat. He stood for a moment gazing round the bar room, then made his way toward the batwings, lamplight glinting on bronzed features.

On the porch, he inhaled deeply, then reached for a cigar. His hand was steady as a rock. And why should it be otherwise?

It was a little after midnight and a strong wind snaked along Trail and lifted the dust. He inhaled deeply and at last the tensions were gone, and with them that unfamiliar self-doubt along with the strange sweet sadness that had dogged him recently. Once again all the loose ends had been drawn together and he was all of a piece. All his uncharacteristic depression had taken was a couple of days of self-indulgence with the brandy and the odd headache before the ingrained habits of self-discipline had kicked in and hauled him out of the slump.

His boot-heels sucked in the deep dust as he walked toward the hotel, hat tipped low against the stinging drive of the wind. The moon was a feeble slice high in the sky and only a scatter of brave stars showed through. Apart from the Lady Jane, the Last Hope and the Chuckwagon Hotel, all Chisum seemed asleep. No roistering wild men, no simmering tingle of trouble in the air.

His lips turned upwards in a rare smile which

144

wasn't destined to last any longer than the time it took for him to reach the livery stables. Another man might have easily missed that faint rustle of sound but to the ears of Marshal Matt Gant it came loud and clear.

Instantly he twisted low and drew. 'Who's there?' he shouted. 'Show yourself!'

Crimson gunflame blossomed like some rare desert flower in the blackness as Trail Street rocked to the cannon blast of the shot that tugged at Gant's jacket sleeve. Then the Buntline Special belched out in snarling response and Gant glimpsed the dim figure as it came staggering forward from the deeper shadows.

The ambusher propped and triggered.

Gant dropped to one knee. That second shot was wild, suggesting the drygulcher might have been hit. But he couldn't gamble on that. Down low now, he fanned his hammer. Gunflame poured into the alleymouth for a thunderous handful of seconds before Harley Raingo came lurching into the light, hugging his body as though deathly cold.

The ambusher began to fall and Gant shifted his aim and triggered again at the second figure who suddenly loomed in back of the hard-hit Raingo. Two of the bastards! His six-gun bucked and smoked and the second man cried out and fell, the sound cutting off abruptly as his face smashed into the earth.

Gant came up in a crouch and leapt for the cover of the livery corner.

'Come on out!' he snarled. 'Hands where I can see them!'

There was no response. All there was to be heard was the low moaning of the man lying face down in the dust.

Gant got his back against a wall and waited motionless with a gun arm extended until men began pouring out into the street from the joints. The marshal turned his head to stare down at Harley Raingo. The killer was dead, drilled through the heart. Men came running up from the Lady Jane. He waved them back then strode deliberately into the alley. His eyes accustomed to the half-light by this, he saw the alley was empty but for the burly figure lying at his feet.

He dropped to one knee and turned the groaning man over onto his back. 'I'm croakin'!' the man whispered hoarsely.

It was big Tom Jethro.

'Marshal!'

Gant twisted to see Bragg standing before the drinkers who were staring down at Raingo. 'I'm all right, Sheriff. Make a light!'

Bragg struck a match and came forward warily. 'Judas Priest!' he breathed. 'Tom!'

'They were waiting here to drygulch me,' Gant announced grimly as others gathered round, some scratching vestas into life, holding them aloft with shaking hands. 'They were—'

'I never did, Gant,' Jethro panted. 'I-I was only

146

gonna be with him while Raingo done it. I met him at the Last Hope and knowin' how I hate your guts . . . he told me . . . what he was gonna do. . . .'

The dying man's eyes flared their hatred in the flickering matchlight.

'I-I wanted to see you get it, Gant, but I never . . . I never. . . .'

He choked on blood. The head rolled and all saw the light fade from staring eyes.

'He's gone,' Bragg murmured. 'Damned young fool. What'd he want to go and get himself tangled up with a feller like—'

'Just a minute there, Bragg,' Grover Parnell said suddenly. 'Jethro weren't packin' no piece!'

Gant turned and stared. It was true. Tom Jethro wore neither shell belt nor gun.

The town-tamer felt a chill grip him as he came forward. 'There must be a gun,' he said hoarsely. 'Look for it, damn you!'

They searched. There was no weapon to be found. In the deepening silence that descended, Karl Heath reminded everybody that big Tom Jethro the bare-knuckle brawler, had never been known to carry a weapon.

Gant's face was the color and texture of chalk as he moved out into the light of Trail Street. 'I killed an unarmed man,' he said tonelessly. 'That is murder.'

'Don't be loco, Marshal,' Mel Bragg protested. 'Hell burn it, Tom was lurkin' in there with that dirty

Raingo and they—'

He broke off abruptly as Gant thrust his revolver at him, butt-first. 'Shooting an unarmed man is murder regardless of the circumstances, Sheriff. Arrest me.'

The lawman's jaw fell open with a click. 'Arrest you, Marshal Gant?' He tried to grin. 'You must be jestin'!'

But Matt Gant was never more serious. This was a man for whom the Marshals' Service Manual was the lawman's bible. And in that bible there was no room for excuses, explanations, qualifiers or mitigating circumstances. There was only the remorseless black and white of the law. Either a man was guilty of a crime or he wasn't. And here in the dust of Trail Street, Chisum, the man some called Stoneface Gant had broken the law which he held higher than loyalty or religion. He would show himself no more mercy than he would anybody else who'd shot down an unarmed man.

'I'm waiting, Sheriff,' he said, white-faced and grim.

Bragg gaped round at the staring faces but found no help there. When he finally turned back to the tall town-tamer and saw his unrelenting expression, that loco as it might seem to be, there was no way for him other than to comply.

'All right, Marshal,' he was finally able to get out. 'Iffen you say so. . . .'

'I say so,' Gant rapped, then led the way across the street.

148

The crowd was hushed as they watched them go, with Bragg forced to trot a little to keep up with Gant's lunging pace. And it was not until some time after the jailhouse door had closed with a clang behind them that old Judge Nimrod, standing dishevelled and with shirt-tail hanging out, broke the heavy quiet.

'He finally did it,' the judge summarized, leaning heavily upon his crutch. 'God help him, but he finally made a mistake. . . .'

'Order, order!' Judge Nimrod shouted, then gavelled the crowded meeting hall into silence with the butt of his old pepperbox pistol. He waited solemnly until the muttering and murmuring faded, then snapped his sharp brown eyes at the sheriff.

'Very well, Sheriff Bragg, what is the nature of the matter which brings us here today?'

Bragg gasped. 'Goddammit it, Judge, you know as well as I do that—'

'The business of the court, Sheriff!' Nimrod rapped. 'This is a formal hearing and will be conducted as such.'

The sheriff swallowed, glanced across at the poker-faced man seated at the prisoner's table, then cleared his throat.

'Well, Judge, I guess the court charges Marshal Gant herewith the shootin' of Tom Jethro when Jethro wasn't packin' no gun.'

'How do you plead, Marshal?' Nimrod rapped.

'Guilty!'

A buzz swept the courtroom. In the front row of the public seating, Rebecca Tucker clutched her brother's arm and shook her head in disbelief, staring at Gant's rigid back. In the next seat behind the Tuckers, Senior Marshal Bryce Shankland, who'd staged in from Sacramento City to reach Chisum just half an hour before the hearing began, glanced up at the judge in mute appeal.

But Judge Nimrod's attention was focused exclusively upon the man seated motionless with hands locked together upon the polished table before him.

'Guilty, eh, Marshal Gant?' he said, sounding like a man enjoying himself. 'Well, that should make my job nice and easy, should it not? All I have to do is find the charge substantiated and they can tote you off to Sacramento City and set you up before a full twelve-man jury, by glory!'

'If you please, Judge,' Shankland called, rising to stand. 'I would like to speak on this man's behalf and—'

'Sit down and shut up, Marshal Shankland,' Nimrod shouted, banging his pistol butt upon the bench. 'I know the facts of this case back to front and I don't ever need help when my duty is as plain as it stands here today.'

Red-faced and muttering, Shankland resumed his seat. There was a scatter of guarded smiles around the musty room. It was a rare field day for the judge when he could cut a tall poppy like Shankland down to size.

Nimrod turned back to Gant. 'Yes, indeed, it's a mighty easy job for me to send you up, Marshal Gant. Only thing, I won't be doing that.'

The judge's words took time to get through to Gant. He raised his big head and stared at the unimpressive figure behind the bench. The judge's eyes crinkled mischievously.

'You be a mighty proud man, Marshal Gant. I swear I can't recollect seeing one more full of pride, in truth. You came ridin' into our town with your hard ways and your iron mouth like you owned it. You stomped over most everybody and you fed us so much law and order that we liked to have choked upon it!'

'Look, Judge—'

The gunbutt whacked down upon the bench. 'I have the chair here, Marshal, not you. And I've got things to say and mean to say them, and you are going to sit there and listen. Understood?'

Gant fixed the man with an iron stare. Yet eventually he nodded.

'Good enough.' Nimrod leaned back in his chair and began to speak, addressing the room in general now. 'Like I say, the marshal came here acting like God Almighty. He stirred up everybody and made more enemies in days than any man should make in a lifetime. . . .'

His voice trailed off, he stifled a cough and went on.

'But the truth was this here town needed the Gant kind of medicine more than any of us knew. He dished it out with both hands and we all hated his insides . . . until we could see what he was doing for us. He was cleaning out the sludge and turning us into a worthwhile place to be, whether we liked it or not. Yessir, he's a strong man with just one big fault. His law had no bends in it . . . and that's what nearly brought him down. The law can't be that way. It has to be able to bend, maybe at times, even break a little. . . .'

He was staring directly at the marshal as he continued.

'The law was never infallible, Mister Gant, and if you don't know that by this, then I'm here to teach you. We saw demonstrated right here how it can make errors. The law found young Jimmy guilty of murder, but as it turned out, the boy was innocent. So, if the law isn't the god you would have us believe, then it's got to be something else. Right? Right. And what the law is, Mister Marshal, is a tool that plain folks use to make their lives better, not turn it into something that rules them. People are the law, sir, and the law is people . . . not just a whole mess of rules written down in a book!'

It was silent in the big room as the judge paused to take a swallow of water from a jug. There was not a man present, Gant included, who was not deeply impressed by his advocacy of the law he believed in.

Nimrod cleared his throat and his manner became brisk.

'All right, with that off my chest, we come to the matter at hand, the shooting of Tom Jethro. Well, I guess we all know the facts well enough. Harley Raingo came here to gun the marshal down from ambush, and big Tom, who'd been roughed up by the marshal more than once himself, elected to go along to watch.'

He paused and spread his gnarled hands as though inviting them all to witness the picture he was painting.

'The marshal was walking along the street at midnight and Raingo tried to shoot his head off. Instead, he gunned Raingo, saw another man just behind him in the darkness and let him have it. Human error, you might call it, yet that is what we are dealing with here. Human beings . . . not bloodless rules in a book. I'd have shot Jethro myself if I'd been in the marshal's boots that night, and if there is any man here who says he would have done any different, then he's nothing but a liar. Charge dismissed! Court dismissed!'

And banged his gavel down with great force.

Gant was on his feet, a protest on his lips. But the judge had already quit the bench and was swinging away on his crutch. Gant whirled to face the crowd, and it was only when he saw them nodding and smiling his way that he slowly realized what had happened here today. And for the first time in his rigid, rule-book life, he fully understood the difference between the hard and unyielding word of the law, and the beautiful human word that was justice.

Seated with Shankland on the upper balcony of the Chuckwagon Hotel, Matt Gant bent forward to watch Sheriff Mel Bragg walk by below. A passing cowpuncher tipped his ragged hat to the peace officer and Bragg nodded gravely.

The chair creaked as Gant leaned back.

'Looks to me like we're going to make it here, after all, Marshal,' Shankland remarked, studying his profile. 'In fact I'm sure of it. You've done a fine job.'

Gant shrugged and the senior marshal went on. 'You sure you won't change your mind and come back to Sacramento City with me?'

Gant shook his head. 'I was only going back to turn in my badge, Marshal. But you have it already, so there's no need for that.'

'But I still can't believe you could just turn your back on what I believe I would be justified in calling your obsession.'

'A hard word, but the right one, sir. Obsession. And it took what unfolded here for me to understand that any obsession will surely kill you in the end . . . unless you know when to say enough.' He spread his hands. 'I'd never find a better time to quit, and I have.'

The senior man knew when he was beaten.

'All right . . . so what are your plans? You spoke once about taking up a section of land, when and if

154

you ever quit. . . .'

'Could have that in mind. Not sure. . . .'

Shankland smiled as he got to his feet and fitted his hat to his head.

'I know one thing you're sure about. You've been through hell here and it's going to take quite a time for you to get everything settled in your mind.' The man walked to the doorway, paused. 'Maybe I'll see you before you go, Marshal?'

'Matt.'

'Oh, yeah . . . that will take some getting used to I guess . . . for everybody. Well, Matt, take it easy and good luck – whatever you decide to do.'

Gant listened to the steps fade along the hallway and murmured, 'Whatever you decide to do. . . .'

He went to the balcony and looked at the big sky. It was late afternoon with a soft breeze stirring the peppercorn trees on the north side of town. He returned to the bench then and sat with closed eyes, allowing all the iron tensions to begin easing out of him. It was all over at last and he was sharply conscious of one door of his life closing and another opening.

But opening to what?

At times he'd dreamed of this day when he would finally be a free agent and a man without obsession once again, but had never expected it would come so abruptly. What did a man do when he severed himself from the life that had dominated every waking moment for the best part of ten years?

He must have dozed for his next awareness was of a presence close by. He jolted awake, right hand going automatically to the Buntline Special. Then he relaxed, pleasantly surprised when he saw who it was.

He got up. Fast.

'Miss Tucker. I thought you'd gone back to the ranch.'

Stunning in the same full-skirted green dress she'd worn to the courthouse hearing, the young woman smiled, then moved across the balcony to stand with her back to the railing.

'We did start for home, Marshal, but then we realized there was something we'd forgotten.'

'Business?'

'I suppose you might call it that.' A pause. 'You look tired.'

'Not really.' His tone was curt. Right now, she was the last person he wished to see, considering the strange uncomfortable battle he'd been fighting with himself to keep her from his thoughts for days on end. Now, seeing her standing before him so young and lovely, with blue sky behind her golden head, the town-tamer felt something akin to a pain he could not explain. But he was sure of one thing: he'd had enough of pain and right at that moment suddenly felt like the weariest man in Mescalero County.

'Marshal Gant—' she began, but he cut her off.

'I'm no longer a marshal, Miss Tucker.' He paused, then heard himself add, 'My name is Matt.'

'Well, now we are finally Matt and Rebecca, that's

an improvement. Whenever you call me Miss Tucker I feel a hundred years old.'

'There was something you wanted to see me about, Miss ... I mean, Rebecca?' he asked, and could hear the formality in his tone.

'Yes, I believe there was something . . . but now I'm standing before you I'm not sure if—'

'Is this to do with the time your brother spent in prison? If so, I can tell you he's liable for compensation for—'

'No,' she cut in. 'It's not about Jimmy.' She paused to study him, then continued quickly. 'It's just that Jimmy and I were wondering if you might care to spend a few days on the Lazy K with us?'

He stared at her so long she began to feel uncomfortable.

'Have I offended you, Matt? I certainly didn't intend to.'

'No,' he said quickly. 'I-I was just surprised. Or maybe astonished is a better word.' He looked genuinely puzzled. 'Why would you of all people want me to come visiting after all I put you through?'

'Well, for one, you obviously need a rest. And the sheriff happened to mention your hinting you might take up ranching when you retired.' She half-smiled, unsure of his reaction. 'We thought we could give you the opportunity to see if you really cared for the life . . . or otherwise. . . .'

He had a feeling of unreality. 'But this doesn't even start to make sense. I tried my damnedest to hang your brother. And I would have done so hadn't—'

'Matt,' she said in a firm strong voice now, 'shall I tell you the real honest-to-God reason why we want you to come home with us for awhile?'

Although still puzzled, he nodded, and the girl took in a deep breath.

'Jimmy and I realize that the three of us have all shared a terrible experience together. And I don't just mean the past week. I'm talking about my father. Jimmy and I suffered terribly at his hands, and it was this that drew us so closely together. You also suffered because of our father, Matt, for he almost crippled you, and did his best to do so. We believe it was because of this hate he engendered in you, that brought you into our lives. Are you starting to understand now? Shep Tucker hurt the three of us cruelly and unnecessarily, so won't you give us the chance to undo at least some of what he did to you?'

Gant could not speak right away. He placed his hand upon the railing and felt something twisting within like a key in a rusted lock. He was the man they called the stone marshal, and yet a slip of a girl had seemed to unlock with just a few simple words of understanding. She had looked beyond the mask he wore of a man lonely and embittered, but now the cause of his bitterness was gone she was pleading with him to let go . . . to give the real Matt Gant a chance to change his life.

Suddenly, astonishingly, he met her eyes and knew

in the instant that he did want to travel to the Lazy K with them, craved it more than anything in his life before. And yet he could imagine the possibility of even greater pain should he accede to her suggestion, for in this hour when Matt Gant was coming to understand who he was and what had driven him so clearly, he could envision an even greater hurt for him when he realized that from the very first, she had been more than just a pretty woman to a lonely man of the gun . . . impossibly much more. . . .

And knew as clearly as he'd ever known anything, that he must not accept this kindness unless he knew there might be, at some distant time in the uncertain future, some glimmer of hope no matter how faint, that – 'What are you dreaming, Gant?' the back of his mind nagged. 'That she might one day come to see you as a man with a heart . . . not just an iron man of the guns?'

It was impossible . . . and yet he heard his own voice now. 'What you just said, Rebecca . . . is that the only reason you want me to visit the ranch? To rest up and—'

She met his gaze in a way he would never forget . . . nor her soft words. 'No, Matt it certainly was not the only reason.' Her eyes sparkled like sunlight. 'Certainly not the most important one.'

That was all that was said. But her eyes said so much more than Matt Gant, the lonely gun, might have dared hope for. Awkwardly, stiffly, he reached out and took her hands in his own. Her fingers were soft and cool and there were tears in her eyes that somehow said far more than mere words ever could.

Then the businesslike voice of Jimmy sounded from down below. 'Hey, Sis, you still up there?'

She squeezed Gant's hand then leaned over the railing. 'Coming now, Jimmy!'

'Is the marshal comin' too?'

'Yes.'

'Told you that you could talk him round!'

She turned back to Gant and slipped her hand through his arm.

'Come on, Matt,' she said, in a way he would never forget. 'Let's go home.'